# THE PASSION FLOWER MASSACRE

## NICOLA MORGAN

Hodder
Children's
Books

A division of Hachette Children's Books

Copyright © 2005 Nicola Morgan

First published in Great Britain in 2005 by Hodder Children's Books

The right of Nicola Morgan to be identified as the Author of the Work has been asserted by her in accordance with the Copyright, Designs and Patents Act 1988.

3

A Catalogue record for this book is available from the British Library

ISBN-10: 0 340 87734 0
ISBN-13: 978 0340877340

Typeset in Bembo by Avon DataSet Ltd, Bidford-on-Avon, Warwickshire

Printed and bound in Great Britain by Bookmarque Ltd, Croydon, Surrey

The paper and board used in this paperback by Hodder Children's Books are natural recyclable products made from wood grown in sustainable forests. The manufacturing processes conform to the environmental regulations of the country of origin.

Hodder Children's Books
A Division of Hachette Children's Books
338 Euston Road
London NW1 3BH

Visit Nicola Morgan's websites: www.nicolamorgan.co.uk
www.childliteracy.com

# THE PASSION FLOWER MASSACRE

## NICOLA MORGAN

Hodder
Children's
Books

A division of Hodder Headline Limited

Losing My Religion Words and Music by Michael Mills, William Berry,
Peter Buck and Michael Stipe © 1991 Night Garden Music, USA
Warner/Chappell Music Ltd, London W6 8BS
Lyrics reproduced by permission of IMP Ltd
All Rights Reserved.

Copyright © 2005 Nicola Morgan

First published in Great Britain in 2005 by Hodder Children's Books

The right of Nicola Morgan to be identified as the Author
of the Work has been asserted by her in accordance with the
Copyright, Designs and Patents Act 1988.

3 5 7 9 10 8 6 4 2

A Catalogue record for this book is available from the British Library

ISBN 0 340 87734 0

Typeset in Bembo by Avon DataSet Ltd,
Bidford-on-Avon, Warwickshire

Printed and bound in Great Britain by
Bookmarque Ltd, Croydon, Surrey

The paper and board used in this paperback by Hodder Children's
Books are natural recyclable products made from wood grown in
sustainable forests. The manufacturing processes conform to the
environmental regulations of the country of origin.

Hodder Children's Books
A Division of Hodder Headline Limited
338 Euston Road
London NW1 3BH

Visit Nicola Morgan's websites: www.nicolamorgan.co.uk
www.childliteracy.com

*For Harry, With Love*

*Part One*

**The Year 2029**

# 1

## Prison – Three Weeks
## Before Release

You had to be tough to do this, thought the little old woman as she looked up at the walls, hard and strong and cold and brutal. You had to have a touch of hardness yourself, when you spoke to the misguided souls inside. Prison was not supposed to be easy, she knew, but she had enjoyed playing her part in helping the occupants, making them ready for the world again. You had to do your best, your very best at all times, to make sure that they would commit no more crimes when they left.

You had to keep a part of yourself back, too, sometimes hide your true thoughts. Honesty is not always the best policy. Sometimes there is a higher aim.

To this higher aim, she would dedicate her remaining life. With passion.

A prison visitor she was, this old woman. Or Volunteer Friend, as they called them these days. Once a week, on a Tuesday, this gentle-faced little old woman with her neat suit and her expensive handbag and her shoes from an exclusive shop in London, braved the cold sheer walls of Dartmoor prison. A thousand square eyes watched as she drove up in her battered red sports car. She had come to know those walls, to find comfort in their brooding strength and the way they kept their secrets, to love the raw liver colour of their bricks and how they sucked poison from the body of the world and swallowed it.

What did those walls contain? What was the poison? A distillation of evil? Or madness? Sadness? Hopelessness? But there was hope, too. For most would go free in the end.

It was one such man she came to visit each Tuesday. She wished she could come more often. She was gripped by this man, she was, this little old woman. And what he had done. But she must try not to think about that. She ought to focus on his battered soul, his guilt, his desire for forgiveness. And how he would soon be free. Her fingers twitched at this thought. Free as a bird he would fly and she would help him go.

For twenty-five years he had been locked away. His crime? Mass murder.

No one knew that he had become her obsession. The other prisoners whom she used to visit had only been a rehearsal for this one soul, the one soul she really wanted to save. What he had done went too far. Perhaps even beyond the bounds of God's forgiveness. If God chose not to forgive him after all, she would not blame Him.

A few minutes later the old woman was entering the prison, passing her fingers over the security scanner that would let her in. She did not need to read the sign telling her to look at the iris-recognition system and wait for the green light to flash. A disembodied sing-song voice spoke: 'Good afternoon, Mrs Bailey. Come through, please.' The door slid into nowhere and, after a pleasant few words with the nice young man at the Control Centre, and a cheery wave from several of the pastel-suited Rehab officers, and a gentle stroke of the Facilitator's cat, she was on her way, along the familiar corridors painted a calming blue and exuding aromatic relaxing air from vents in the floor. She followed the yellow-clad female Rehab officer, who was young enough to be her granddaughter.

Not that she had a granddaughter.

As the door slid open, her heart spun and her breath caught fleetingly on something spiky in her throat. It always did, each time she saw his face. His gentle, soft-seeming face with its pale blue eyes and long hair. Hair that used to be corn-gold – she had seen the pictures on the news and in all the papers twenty-five years ago.

Now his hair was greying at the edges, but still it looked like a halo, it did. Always his hair had looked like a halo.

He really did look like the pictures of Jesus.

You could see why so many people were taken in. He just looked like every jumped-up Messiah who had ever believed he was God's gift to the world. A worm of hatred began to uncurl in her stomach. No! She must keep her true thoughts locked away. She must not judge. It should be for God to judge, it should. She must remember that. This was a man who, they said, was sorry for what he had done. Who had only acted through madness and now was cured.

The psychiatrist had confirmed it. A nice woman. Rather young perhaps, but she seemed to know what she was doing. Other psychiatrists had said the same over the years, each time his case came up for release. But each time, the politicians had responded to the outcry from the public, the Internet chat-coms, the huge flashing text-message boards that occupied every public space nowadays, the crowds of ugly strangers with their noisy electronic placards, who shouted and ranted about a life for a life, who hurled abuse and stones at the prison van each time he had a court appearance. Eventually, however, his lawyers and psychiatrists had won, and he would be freed.

Only three weeks from now.

Just when she was getting to know him properly, this little old woman with her nicely-tailored clothes and her carefully-cut fingernails, almond-shaped, in the old-fashioned style. And her hair that sat, just so, still and obedient. Just when she thought he was about to tell her everything, to reveal himself to her. She wanted that, needed to see the core of him – whether it was badness or madness, she didn't much care, but she wanted to know it. She wanted to hear how he would justify himself to God when the time came. Then God could judge. This she had promised. And if Peter had suffered too, then reliving that suffering would be his atonement. Part of his payment.

To begin, today, as always, they chatted. About this and that. He grew flowers. His sweet peas were in bloom now. He wanted to show her. Perhaps the Rehab officer would show her his sweet peas in the garden on her way out. He was looking forward to growing raspberries again when he was freed, he said. And tayberries. Blueberries to make smooth jelly. And tiny sweet green Muscat grapes in a greenhouse.

'So, you will definitely start your fruit farm again, will you?' she asked. It was the fruit farm where it had all happened.

'Well, not the same one as before, of course.' He smiled sadly. That delicate shiver of a half-smile that

came right from the heart and pierced anything in its
way.

No, of course, not the same one, she thought. That
would hardly be possible.

The smell of burning raspberry canes hit her nostrils.
The sickly stench of wet charred straw and roasted . . .
She swallowed.

There was a silence. He massaged the palm of one
hand, then the other. As though he was in pain. Or as
though he was trying to rub something away.

'I will miss our chats,' he said. He brushed a strand of
hair from his eyes. She always noticed how long his
fingers were, and soft and slow like feathers. Yes, she
could see why women, younger women, fell for his
charms. And his voice, his smooth vanilla voice.

'Yes, so will I,' said the old woman, fingering the
diamond chunk on her wedding finger. 'But you must
move on, you know. You must move on. You have
been given a second chance.'

'But have I been forgiven? That's what I need to
know. That's what I really need to know.' She heard a
catch in his voice. Looked at him. He was looking away,
towards the swimming-pool-blue square that was the
window, like an abstract painting she had once seen that
was just a blue square, no texture, no anything but flat,
plain, bland, empty, meaningless blue. It had meant

nothing to her, at the time, that painting. It meant everything now, in here. It meant the world. It meant heaven.

She saw that at the corner of one eye glistened a tear. He wiped it away.

'Have I been forgiven, Sarah? I sense you would know. There is something special about you.' And he reached towards her hands as they rested on the table. Her dry, worn hands, her sad hands. He could tell they were sad hands. They reminded him of his mother's. Though his mother did not have diamond rings like that. If she had, she would have given them to the poor. Because his mother was good and knew everything there was to know about rich men and camels and heaven and the eyes of needles.

A small buzzer sounded. They looked towards the glass window in the wall. A Rehab officer wagged a finger. No touching. He must keep his hands to himself. Not that he had actually touched her – she had not moved her hands. He rubbed his palms again. Massaged away the pain, real or imaginary.

'Oh, yes. I am sure you have been forgiven,' she said, blandly, glibly. 'God forgives all who turn to Him, remember? And God loves you, of course. You know that, don't you?' She made herself think it, so that it came out with the sound of truth. Perhaps it was true?

God moves in mysterious ways, she reminded herself. Not for her to reason why.

'I don't know,' he said. 'I don't know.' There was silence as he seemed to wrestle with something inside himself. 'Sarah?'

'Yes?'

'Do you have children? I never asked before.'

She shook her head, hiding her thoughts. She did not trust herself to answer that one with words. With words that might spit and strangle their way from her and split her heart in two. She would not talk about that.

'If you did . . .' He paused. 'If you did, would you . . .' He stood up.

'What is it, Peter? What is it?'

'I want to tell you something. I did tell the psychiatrists but they didn't say much. Let me tell you. So you will see why it all happened. So you will see it was not my fault. Not really. Although, of course, I take the blame.'

He will manipulate you, they had told her. He will try to make you think he is an angel. He is no angel – he was a sick man and now he is healed. That is all. But don't listen to everything he says. With his warped memory, he probably *believes* everything he says.

He could not manipulate her. She was stronger than that. She might look like a plain little old woman but there was an inner strength to her. No one knew how strong she was inside. You had to be tough, to do this, to do what she was doing. It was hot work on the edge of hell.

But this was what she had been waiting to hear. Why he thought he could justify what he had done. Why did he become the man — mad or bad — that he became? And if he *did* try to manipulate her, that would only test her, strengthening her.

And, of course, she had promised his confession to God. It was for God to judge. Of course.

He began to speak. Another small tear drying in one corner of his eye.

And as he spoke, eloquently, softly, sadly, she felt she could picture the scene exactly.

*The son, a small boy, four years old, crouched in the corner of the cellar. He hugged his arms around his knees. His wet sheet was in a bundle in the corner. He would not look at it. It was his fault. He could smell the stale urine on his pyjamas. He had been in the cellar for two hours and in the mildewed air the wetness refused to dry.*

*As he crouched and hugged himself, he rocked and prayed, just as he had been taught. If he prayed hard enough he would be forgiven.*

*But he could not pray hard enough because one bad part of*

his mind was listening for footsteps. Because he could not pray hard enough, he would be punished.

There they were. His heart quickened and he almost choked on a breath. The smell of urine rose and grew and stuck in his throat. The sound of a key grated in the lock. The door opened and light flooded in. The mother and father came in. The son stood up, the cold air clammy on his damp pyjamas.

'Take off your clothes.' Fumbling, desperate to please, he obeyed.

'The sheet.' He wrapped the wet sheet around his naked body, trying not to shiver in the cold and fear.

The father went over to the corner of the room. With difficulty, he lifted the familiar wooden structure from the floor and leaned it against the wall. The mother moved to help him. The father steadied it and the mother helped the son climb on to it. She smiled. The son stifled a small sob.

Together, the mother and the father gently and lovingly fastened the ropes to bind the son's wrists and ankles to the limbs of the cross.

Then the mother and the father knelt and prayed. Knife-like pain shot through their knees, but still they prayed. Their muscles went into spasm, but they did not stop praying. Their fingers and bare feet became cold and then numb, but still they never stopped loving their only son and praying.

★ ★ ★

The little old woman sat in her tattered red sports car, a once aspirational Branson Mirage. With her hands on the mouldable squishtic steering-wheel, she leaned back in the seat and breathed out slowly.

It was a beautiful story.

She smiled.

It was a beautiful and terrible story. But it was not enough, surely? It was like saying one Hail Mary when more were needed. If Peter wanted God's forgiveness, he surely needed to have suffered much more. Atonement could not be so easy.

Surely God would want her to do more? And she had, of course, promised his soul to God.

The fact that she, too, wanted to see inside him and to know it all was entirely irrelevant, of course.

Peter leaned back on his bed and smiled peacefully to himself. Nearly there. So nearly there. In three more weeks he would be free. And now, just in time, there was a stupid little old woman who cared enough about him to listen to him. There had been other Volunteer Friends before her, but none of them had been the right one.

Not that he cared at all about the old woman. Only her money. Those rings must be worth a fortune. And he had seen her wear at least four different jewelled brooches in the last few weeks. You could tell by the way she dressed that she had money. Even her hairstyle, old womanish though it was. Smooth. Like a silver rolling mist. None of the nicotine tinge of a poor old woman's hair. And she had no children, she'd said. Crucially, beautifully, perfectly, she had no children. No children to interfere or for her to leave her idle money to.

When he got out of here, he would need money. So that he could start it all over again. So that he could walk in strawberry fields again. So that he could do what God had put him on this earth to do.

To save souls and speed them to heaven. And the stupid old woman would help him. She would have no choice. She had come into his life and he would not let her go.

Until it was time.

As before. With the others.

*Part Two*

# The Year 2004

# 1

## B is for Beginning

They should never have done the journey in one go. Should have stayed the night somewhere on the way. Then they could have arrived in daylight. They would have been full of energy instead of tired and irritable. And they would have seen the swelling hills of Devon in sunshine.

Then it could all have been exactly as Matilda had expected. She had pictured every detail. It would be a fruit farm with neat rows of raspberry canes and redcurrant bushes and lines of strawberry plants ribboning the hillsides. She'd imagined tired but happy workers finishing their day, juice smeared on faces, sun-streaked hair, a healthy apple glow on every cheek. Laughter, cider, barbecues. A decent choice of talent, all muscle and suntan.

That was how she had dreamed of freedom. Leaving home. Two weeks after leaving school, her childhood behind her now. The cold Edinburgh houses were a dull memory and the warmth of the West Country was her new home for the next three months. A hot romantic Dartmoor summer of fruit-picking spread ahead of her, before her exciting gap year trip to Chile. Life. Real life. Making her own rules. Escape from everything that had held her back. Escape from memories too painful to hold on to.

Instead of which, here she was, arriving late at night after an eleven-hour drive. She had dozed off several times towards the end, slumped uncomfortably on the back seat against a lumpy heap of bags. Each time, she had been woken by Jack opening the driver's window wide to let the cold night air in. The first time she had snapped at him, but he had retorted, 'Yeah, well, if you'd spent more time taking driving lessons instead of letting your parents drive you around in their swanky Jag, you might be sharing the driving, and then I wouldn't be so tired, would I? What would you rather? You get a little bit cold or I fall asleep and crash the car?' And there was no answer to that. Cally couldn't drive either, but she had at least started to learn. Besides, Cally was Jack's girlfriend and therefore protected. Beautiful, delicate, perfect Cally. If she wasn't her best friend, Matilda would probably have hated her.

And so the journey had been an ordeal. Instead of an

exhilarating drive to freedom, it had been slow, sticky and stressful. Instead of the hot summer's wind beating on her face and hair through the open sun-roof of her dad's Jaguar, the windows had to be shut so that Jack and Cally could listen to their music. Instead of riding high in her mum's safe, air-conditioned Audi, they had sweated in an airless, crumby Ford-something that had to stop every hour or the engine overheated. She had imagined smelling strawberries when she arrived. Instead, she smelled only her own sweat and the rank petrolly stink of a cheap car.

But here they were. Apple Tree Farm. When she'd seen the name in the advert she'd thought of Enid Blyton books. Picnics, clean cows mooing softly in a nearby field, hazy sunshine and bumble-bees buzzing. Home-baked apple cake made with home-grown apples from the orchards. And lashings and lashings of ginger beer. Or preferably not ginger beer but something more interestingly alcoholic.

Now Apple Tree Farm just sounded like a cliché. A con. How could she have been so naïve? This so-called farm was a commercial venture. She could tell that from the car park and the Swiss-style log cabin café and the neat metal fences everywhere. Even in the dark, she could see that this was no old-fashioned farm. There probably wouldn't even be a farm cat.

A farm cat would be against the rules of health and safety.

They already knew they were too late to get into the workers' hostel. They could see the sign to it, up a tidy tarmac track past the shop and café. But their instructions had been clear when they'd been offered the job. The doors were locked at eleven-thirty pm. It was now well after midnight. They would have to sleep in the car.

Matilda's first night of freedom was a definite disappointment. As she crouched in the cold darkness to pee behind a tree, she scowled. There was nowhere to wash. Her teeth were fur-coated, her armpits sticky and her hair lank already. She stank. She climbed back into the car in silence. As she tried to make herself comfortable on the back seat, pushing the bags as far away as possible, she saw Jack's hand reach across to hold Cally's in the passenger seat. She saw Cally turn to him and smile. And then she had to watch their faces move together for a slow kiss.

Stinking breath, she thought to herself. But that did not stop the pang of loneliness. If she didn't have Cally and Jack because they had each other, who did she have for herself?

She recognised the shadow inside her. It was creeping forwards, spreading out. It always did that when she was feeling down. She had learned to control it, sometimes, and she would control it now. You controlled it by looking away, looking ahead, not behind. Because the shadow must always stay behind you. If you walk towards the light, the shadow stays behind you. And if you never look back at it, and if you keep the light bright in front of you, the shadow can't creep up and get you.

She pushed her mind to other places. To freedom and dreams.

Then suddenly she remembered. She had promised to phone her parents when she arrived. It was probably too late now, but she could text. Her phone had been off to save the battery so she switched it on now and found that her father had already texted her, irritatingly, an hour ago: 'Where are you? Have you arrived? We are worried. Please contact us. Dad x' He never did abbreviations in texts. Couldn't bring himself to break so many rules all in one go. Rules make life simple and stop the need to think. And where her father led, her mother generally followed. It was easier that way. A united front, rigid and strong. Do not drop your guard, in case emotion enters.

And in her father's case, that guard must never, never, be dropped. Her father, the tower, built tall and utterly unbreakable. Her mother a Rapunzel, hiding herself in its comforting prison.

She texted them now. 'Arvd. Slow jrny. Fine. Mx' She turned the phone off again and closed her eyes.

# 2

## D is for Dream

Always the same dream. It was always raining but the rain was warm. She was outside a house. The walls of the house were thick, thick as castle walls, and as old, the air inside cold and still and smelling of death. She knew that, even though she was outside. She wanted to tell the people inside, to tell them to leave, to make them run away from the death smell and come into the warm rain with her. And she always began by knocking gently on the window, so as not to disturb them or frighten them, but just to tell them softly, to rescue them with a whisper. But they could not hear. So she would begin to knock harder. Not to whisper any more but to speak ever more loudly. Almost to shout. And her fingers would begin to hurt. And she would worry about breaking the window.

Still they would not hear. She could not hear what they were saying either and she wanted to; she so wanted to. There was the man and the woman and the boy. The boy lay in a bed, his hollowed, haunting face white against the pillow. The woman was sitting reading to him and the man had hunched himself over in a chair at the other side, holding the boy's hand in silence.

The woman was beautiful, dressed as though for a smart dinner, as though she had been going out and then had decided to stay with her sick child. Her dying son. And the man, too, so handsome in his black dinner jacket and the red bow tie. But he had pulled his bow tie loose, because he was going nowhere any more, and it fell limply around his neck.

There were tears in the beautiful woman's eyes and she wiped her cheek with the back of a hand heavy with diamonds. And the man reached a hand over to her and held hers. And then they each held a hand of their dying son, as the woman read from the book that leaned against the boy's spiderously thin body. The words she read were wasted, leaking continuously from her mouth, only there to plug a void and to stop the scream rising inside her.

In her dream, Matilda knew the woman was her mother, but it wasn't the mother she knew. It was a dream mother. The mother her real mother probably wished she was. In *her* dreams too. It was as if, while dreaming, Matilda could see the secret wishes in her mother's heart, as if they dreamed the same dreams and there was no barrier of flesh and blood between them, no barrier of real life. In the dream, this made sense and felt true. It was only when she tried to work it out in words afterwards that it slipped into vapour and confusion. It is easy to know in dreams.

Dreaming still, Matilda knew that this was the warm mother her mother dreamed of being.

And her father? She did not know. This man was breaking but her real father never had or would or could. It must not be the same one.

A fire burned in the grate. The room became a Dickensian cliché, the windows suddenly etched with snowy drifts, firelight bouncing off the family silver, inky smoke drifting upwards from an oil lamp.

In the corner of the room lay the shadow. It grew and swelled and spread like oil from the ground. In her dream Matilda could see it creep towards the bed. She hit the window hard now, began to shout, to scream, to tell them that they must get out. That they must come with her and run away. That they must leave the dying boy behind in the bed, that the shadow was going to get him anyway but that they could save themselves and come with her into the laughing rain.

And then, when she thought that surely the window

must break, as the shadow crept around their feet beside the bed, as the darkness slunk up the legs of the bed towards him, the boy looked at her, straight at her through the cracking glass, and smiled. The man and woman never saw as he grinned at her and whispered softly, 'Matilda, it's time. Come with me, Matilda. Come with me, Matty.'

Every time, every time in her dream she ran away. Never did she go with her dream-brother. Every time she ran through the warm rain. Every time, as she ran, her heart ached and swelled and cracked inside her. And although when it cracked it felt like relief, at the same time the emptiness was even worse than the ache. And every time, when she stopped, she refused at first to look back. She stood there, knowing that she must look back because something told her that she must. Something was back there and she would have to look at it because you have to look if you want to know. You do want to know. You always do. And she looked back, and every time, there was nothing there. No house. No mother, no father, no dying boy.

Just a dark shadow creeping through the emptiness. And the understanding, too late, that she should not have looked at it. Because now it would always be there. In her dream, she knew that with a sunlit brilliance. A too-late flash of clarity.

Every time, she woke with warm rain running down her face.

This time, as she woke, glassy dawn light was filtering through the car windows. It took several moments before she realised properly where she was. She looked at her watch. Just after five. As the dream faded, she wiped her eyes and forced the sadness away. It was only a dream. And she knew what it meant, anyway. One day she would be free of it. She had been told that. One day she would be free of it all. But it seemed as though the dream came more often now, not less. It was hard to believe that she was getting better. One doctor had even told her that it would get better when she left home and became independent. She would start to let go of the past.

Anyway, here she was. Nearly five hundred miles from her parents. Starting a new life. With her two best friends. The sky was a watery pink around the rising sun. And today maybe she would smell the strawberry fields.

She was hungry. Very. Cally and Jack were still asleep.

Someone was coming towards them. A girl – woman – long blond hair swinging loose, walking down the track from the hostel. At the same time, a milk van pulled up noisily beside the car and hooted aggressively.

A man leaned out of the window, 'Oy, you'll need to move this, mate.'

'Jack! Wake up! You need to move the car.' She tapped him on the shoulder and he began to stir.

Groggily, Jack turned the key and the car stuttered awake. He moved it a couple of metres so that it wasn't blocking the gateway, and the milk van clattered through.

Cally was awake now, too. Outside, the girl was nearly at the car. She couldn't be a fruit-picker, thought Matilda, not wearing that white shirt and the palest blue jeans.

They wound down their windows. Matilda shivered in the cold. 'Can I help you?' the girl asked. She seemed ridiculously wide awake for such an early hour.

Matilda spoke. 'Hi, we're meant to start work today. We arrived too late for the hostel last night? You should have our . . .'

'Sure, welcome. Are you Matilda or Carolyn?' She smiled in a friendly way and held out her hand.

'I'm Matilda, and this is Cally. And this is Jack.' The girl's handshake through the window was firm, and lingering. She held on a little too long, Matilda thought, and stared into their eyes just a little too deeply. She only looked about eighteen, the same as Matilda, but had an extra stillness, a clear confidence. Beautiful, too, her skin clear and smooth as a model's, Matilda noticed, wishing she looked a bit better herself.

'Hi, I'm so pleased to meet you,' said the girl. 'I'm Maggie. You must be starving. And I expect you'd like to shower. You can drive the car up to the hostel. They'll be up by now so just ring the bell and tell them who you are. I'll see you around. Have a good day,' and she walked towards the shop, taking some keys out of a tight jeans pocket as she did.

Jack watched her go.

'Hey, goggle-eyes!' said Cally, nudging him. 'Take your eyes off her and get me to food and a hot bath. I'm starving and you stink.'

# 3

## G is for Gooseberry and Gorgeous and George

The hostel was busy with bodies waking, washing, eating, shouting. The smell of feet, sweat, coffee and burnt toast. People shouting at each other to get out of the showers or the toilets. Too many people in too small a space.

A girl who introduced herself as Jules showed them where to put their bags. There were four dormitories, two for girls and two for boys, each with about ten metal beds and institutional dark-grey blankets tangled with sleeping-bags. Jules showed them where to shower. 'Don't take too long,' she called. 'Or you'll be late for breakfast.' But Matilda stood under the jets of hot water for a minute longer anyway, feeling the grit and grease wash away.

Only ten minutes later, she was with the others in the dining-room, enjoying the fantastic taste of a bacon roll oozing tomato ketchup, washed down by a mug of strong tea. She looked round the room. Normal people, she thought. They seemed nice, friendly. Several had said hello. The atmosphere felt relaxed. She could enjoy herself here.

Outside, the early sun was glancing through the windows and the sky was already a light butterfly blue.

A bell rang, and everyone suddenly moved to finish and clear away their dishes. A cry of 'Ten minutes!' and within a minute the dining-room had emptied. Matilda, Jack and Cally copied the others, stacking their plates in the hatch and thanking the two steamy-faced girls who worked in the kitchen. Jules shouted to them through the doorway, 'Meet me at the entrance in five minutes. We leave at six sharp. You need water. Sun cream. Oh, and toilet paper.' Toilets? In the fields? Or perhaps not, thought Matilda reluctantly. This had not been part of her too-perfect picture of life on a fruit farm.

They were ready in four minutes. Two open-backed trucks arrived and everyone piled in. A couple of boys were late and ran behind their truck until they could grab onto the back and pull themselves up. Judging by everyone's comments, this was a regular occurrence.

People introduced themselves but Matilda couldn't remember which names went with which faces. She concentrated on smiling and seeming friendly, but couldn't think of anything to say. She let herself simply listen. Jack and Cally stayed close together. Matilda found herself on the other side of the truck from them, squeezed between a large girl with a greasy face and a thin boy with a greasy face. His name was Paul and he kept leering at her as he asked predictable questions about where she was from and how long she was staying. He hadn't cleaned his teeth and he picked at a piece of food stuck somewhere. Why did she have to end up next to him and not the much more gorgeous specimen down the other end? She tried to catch the gorgeous specimen's eye but he was listening to something through earphones.

After a few minutes of bone-shaking ride over rough track and field, they came to a halt by a small Portacabin. At the side of the Portacabin were two toilet cubicles, Matilda noticed with relief.

Everyone clambered out of the trucks. A girl stood with a clipboard. She greeted everyone by name and allocated each to a particular letter of the alphabet. As Matilda watched the workers depart in different directions, she worked out that each section of each field had a letter.

She looked around as she waited in line. Somehow she had expected something very high-tech, with sheds and conveyor belts and people wearing white caps. This all looked very traditional and simple, but maybe that was something to do with it being organic. All things natural and good, as the advert had said.

Matilda stayed close to Cally and Jack, hoping that she would go to the same field as them. She kept her eye on the talent too. Strained her ears to catch his name when he reached the girl. Matt. His name was Matt! It was an omen. And gave her a good reason to speak to him later.

As they stood waiting their turn, Matilda realised something. She almost didn't notice it at first, because everything felt strange, anyway: but after a while, she noticed that the atmosphere around the girl with the clipboard was odd. People who had been smiling and joking before, now stood quietly as they waited for the girl to speak to them. No one made any comment when given a field to go to. No one joked with her, just politely said 'Good morning' when she said 'Good morning'. Only when people were several yards away, walking towards their allotted fields, did they seem to relax and start chatting.

Jules introduced them to the girl. 'Good morning, Rachel. This is Jack and Matilda and Cally. Guys, this is Rachel. She is in charge.' Even Jules was doing it, the serious face, the quiet voice, the obvious respect. It was as though Rachel was much older, held some extra authority. Yet she looked hardly older than them. Like

Maggie, she wore a white shirt and very pale clean jeans so she obviously was not going to be doing dirty work. You couldn't imagine her risking getting tayberry juice on those jeans. You couldn't actually imagine her sweating, either.

Rachel smiled piercingly at them and held out her hand. 'Welcome,' she said, formally. 'It's very good to have you here.' And with each of them she held their hands for fractionally too long, looking deep into their eyes. Matilda smiled back as confidently as she could.

'Now,' said Rachel, looking at her clipboard, 'I've put you all in different fields. I thought it would be a good way for you to get to know people. Jack, section A – that's strawberries. Over there, see?' And she pointed up the hill. 'Sorry, you've got the furthest to go. Cally, section D, strawberries too. Follow Matt – you'll catch him if you're quick. And Matilda, let's see, yes – gooseberries. Section P. Along there, see – just before that row of trees at the bottom of the hill?' Matilda, trying to ignore the feeling of disappointment as she watched Cally run off after Matt, looked towards the hill, squinting in the brightness.

'Ever felt like a gooseberry?' joked Jack, confident enough about Cally not to feel jealousy.

'Christ, trust me to get gooseberries. Who the hell eats gooseberries these days, anyway?'

'Matilda, I'm sorry. I know you are new here, but we don't use that sort of language.' Rachel's face looked friendly and her voice was warm, but there was a coldness in her eyes. Matilda blushed. She felt like a small child. Her parents were bad enough but she thought she'd got away from rules like that. Thought she could decide what words to use and what words not to use. She was eighteen, for Christ's sake. Well, she could at least *think* 'that sort of language'. The girl couldn't read her mind, could she?

But then again, from the way those cool eyes continued to stare into her, perhaps Rachel *could* read minds.

'Sorry,' she muttered. It was a bad start. She wanted to be liked, to make new friends. Well, perhaps not someone like Rachel. But at the same time, she wanted to be respected. And yes, respected by someone like Rachel, however stupid that might sound. Rachel was having a strange effect on her. She was beginning to feel oddly meek. That was the word that came into her head. Meek. She didn't think it was a word she would ever have applied to herself before.

The meek shall inherit the earth.

It was just a thought that slipped unasked into her mind. She knew her Bible. Not for nothing the endless hours spent listening to the dour-faced minister every

Sunday for the first thirteen years of her life. Until she had put her foot down, much to her parents' disapproval. 'Religion forms the backbone of society,' was their view, intoned by one or the other during regular arguments. 'Without it, one has no moral framework. One becomes nothing but a relativist.'

She had learned not to bother to reply.

Matilda began to walk in the direction she'd been shown, towards the gooseberry section. 'You'll need to hurry, Matilda,' came Rachel's voice after her. 'All the best rows will be taken if you don't hurry.'

The best rows of gooseberries. I can't wait, she thought. But she walked quickly anyway.

She was following the lower line of the hill, but her eyes were drawn further up, towards the house squatting at the top. Huge, elegant, regal. The gardens in front of it were laid out in a perfect pattern of squares and rectangles and paths sloping down the hill. Rows of what looked like vegetables. Neat lines, like lines of green print. They reminded her of an alphabet book she had had as a child. It was called *My Garden Alphabet*. A is for apples, and there had been neat rows of apple trees, and she'd had to count the apples and write tidy rows of the letter A in a box. 'B is for bumble-bee buzzing busily. Count the stripes on the bee and write the letter B. Write it neatly, you must. C is for a cuddly cat counting carrots. Can you think of something that rhymes with cat? D is for dirty dog digging daisies. Look! What is the dog burying in the hole? And there'd be a buzzy bee and a cuddly cat and a dirty digging dog, buzzing and purring and barking. As if that was life. And on every page, nature was squashed into the rules of reading, so oranges were organised and perfect peaches queued quietly by rows of round radishes and seven sweet strawberries and ten tasty tomatoes under an umbrella of various vegetables. By which time the worried writer had realised that there are no garden words that begin with X and so had forced something into a box and introduced an axe and a fox somehow, before bringing on the yummy yellow yams with a yawn of exhaustion. And on the last page, of course, the cat and the dog and the bee all fell asleep in a heap with three curly lines of '*zzzzzzzzzzzzzzzzzzzzzzzzzz*' coming from their mouths.

She hated that book. Four years old she was, trying to learn to read. She remembered sitting in her bedroom, alone, at a little wooden desk with a ridge for her perfectly-sharpened pencil to sit in. Her parents were in the next room. Her brother's room. With the doctor. Always she remembered them in her brother's room. With the doctor.

A is for ambulance.

B is for brother. And bed.

C is for cancer. And chemotherapy.

D is for dying.

To the right of the house she could see greenhouses, huge, in a row. A few people walking towards them. She couldn't see their faces from this distance, but she did notice that they all wore white shirts, like Rachel. And Maggie.

She was nearly at the gooseberry section now. She could see the large white placard with the letter P and an arrow. Over to the left, and a little way up the hill, she could see plastic tunnels. A sign pointing in that direction had said 'POLY-TUNNELS'. She couldn't see what was in them, but she assumed they were delicate fruits. Perhaps melons. Or peaches. Or maybe just fragile varieties of strawberries. She didn't really know. They didn't have poly-tunnels in *My Garden Alphabet*.

At the beginning of the gooseberry section, there was a three-sided shed, just tall enough for someone to stand in, with a table and piles of boxes. A guy about her age was standing there. He smiled, asked her name, ticked her off his list. 'You new?'

'Yes.'

'Know what you're doing? With gooseberries?'

'Haven't a clue. I've never done this before.'

'No problem. Everyone's here now so I'll show you. Come with me. Oh, you'll need these,' and he handed her a stack of cardboard cartons with handles. 'I'm George, by the way. You come far?'

He was easy to talk to. Nice-looking. Quite short. Thick hair streaked by the sun, brown eyes, cute suntanned cheekbones. Easy smile. Not her type. Too safe. Maybe a year ago. Not now. Not now she had wings and could fly as close to the sun as she wished.

'Who lives in the house?' Matilda asked, gesturing up the hill.

He looked at her, paused. Hesitated. As if deciding what to say. 'You know Rachel?'

'The girl giving the orders?'

'Yep, that's her. Well, she lives there. And some others.'

'So they work on the fruit farm?'

'They own the fruit farm.'

'What, you mean it's a family?'

'Not in the sense you mean.'

'Oh, and how many senses of "family" are there?' she teased him.

'Look, I don't know, OK. I don't know who they are. But we all know to do what we're told. They're in charge. It's just easier if you play along. Unless you've got another job to go to.'

'Weird. They seem weird. A bit creepy, if you ask me.'

George stopped. He spoke quietly, so she could hardly hear. 'Listen, Matilda, just be careful, really careful what you say, OK? If you want to keep your job, just don't let them hear you saying they're weird. They employ you. They can fire you too. If you want my opinion, yes, they're weird. But I didn't say that and I'll deny it if anyone asks me. There was a girl, Jem . . . Right, Matilda, this is where you can start.' Suddenly his voice had changed, become loud. Matilda knew without looking that someone was coming towards them and, whoever it was, George did not want the person to hear what he had been going to say.

'Good morning,' said a voice.

'Good morning, David,' said George. 'This is Matilda. She's new. I'm just about to show her what to do.' Matilda turned round to face the most gut-crushingly gorgeous guy she had ever seen. There were no words to describe him. It was all in her insides, like warm water. When he shook her hand, holding on just that little bit long, and held her eyes with his, she felt herself dissolve.

'Welcome, Matilda. I hope you are very happy here.' He smiled at her, a Hollywood smile of perfect symmetry. She muttered something like, 'Thanks, yeah, thanks.' Letting her hand go slowly, he turned and walked on.

The summer was looking good. Just as she had hoped. In her best dreams. The daydreams, where the world was perfect and she got everything she wanted. A finger-snapping daydream. A pink champagne and ice-cream daydream. A lottery-winning, money-coming-out-of-your ears, endless wishes daydream. Better than heaven.

Obviously, he was wearing a white shirt. He was one of Them. She had noticed that. Well, maybe weird wasn't so bad after all. Maybe she was just being judgmental before. Judgmental? She was turning into her parents. And she must never do that, she mustn't.

'OK, take me to those gooseberries,' she said, not wanting George to know the effect David was having on her. And as she followed George, she glanced back at David's disappearing back.

He had the tightest ass she had ever seen.

# 4

## S is for Shadow and Sun

Gooseberries were hairy and unpleasant. And they didn't even taste nice. They made your tongue contract and they felt like some kind of watery, crunchy plastic. Why couldn't she have been allowed to pick strawberries on her first day? Or raspberries. Or tayberries. Or why couldn't she be in the polytunnels with the delicate varieties, something sweet and warm? Or in the greenhouses up at the big house, with things like lemons or grapes or whatever they had up there?

Instead, here she was with small, green, hairy things with thick skin that got stuck in your teeth. They didn't even smell sweet. And the leaves stained your fingers green. And they were low down so your shoulders ached. Especially after two hours of it.

She wanted to talk to George. Wanted to ask him to finish whatever he was going to say about a girl called Gem something – Gemma? Jemima? But there were always other people nearby. She decided she would ask him later.

Meanwhile, she tried to stop being bitter about the gooseberries and simply to enjoy the sun on her back. This was freedom, after all. Her parents and their disapproval – unspoken or not – their perpetual worrying, their questions laden with doubt and guilt and caution, were hundreds of miles away. She had left home and she could contact them when she wanted to. If she wanted to. She did not have to be back home by any particular time. She did not have to say where she was going. She did not have to answer questions about who she was with. She did not have to hide the fact that sometimes there was alcohol on her breath after a night out, even though she'd probably only had two or three drinks, or the smell of smoke on her clothes, even though she didn't smoke. Just how many rules did you have to have, simply in order to stay alive, which was her parents' only aim? Just how many risks must be anticipated and avoided? And why? Because they loved her? Or because they could not go through losing her as well?

Now, she did not have to watch her mother's brittle silence or listen to her father's unnecessary anger when he read something that annoyed him from the newspaper. She did not have to listen to the brooding tick of the hall clock through the hollow house. She did not have to see the photographs of her dead brother staring at her from every shelf, every sideboard, every table, every damned ledge. She did not have to be haunted by the shadow in their lives.

She only needed to look ahead, at the light.

As she paused in her gooseberry-picking, and brushed some hair off her damp face, she looked up at the house. She could see David and Rachel walking towards it. Could see some figures waving at them from the garden. Could see the greenhouses glinting in the sun.

Her eyes were caught by some activity to the left of the house. A group of people. Led by a man wearing a long white garment. His hair was long, too, past his shoulders. Blond, almost shining in the sunlight. As he walked, he was followed by several people, all wearing white shirts. He stopped and turned towards them, obviously speaking. And they seemed to listen carefully, stopping too. He reached out his hand and one of the girls took it and held it to her face.

Christ, he looked like Jesus! She almost laughed. That hair! The robe!

The man looked down the hill and spread out his arms. As he did so, a shadow swept down the hillside towards Matilda. So fast that it made her gasp. A sudden coldness reached out to her and her heart began to beat faster, with something that felt like fear, though she didn't know why. She shivered in her T-shirt.

The shadow was still rushing towards her. She wanted to shout but a terrible panic stopped her voice in her throat. She turned away, remembering that she must always keep the shadow behind her. But it was too late. She felt her legs disappear into empty space. Her world went black.

'Matilda! Matilda!' She felt herself come back, spinning through the cold darkness. She was on the ground, crouched on hands and knees. Feeling sick. George was shaking her shoulder. 'Matilda! Wake up! Are you OK?'

He was holding out a bottle of water. 'Here, drink this. You fainted, I think. Probably the sun. Now lie down. Here – in the shade. And bend your legs so your knees are higher than your head. Helps the blood go back to your brain.' She did everything she was told, waiting for her head to clear. She felt stupid and confused.

'Sorry,' she said. 'I . . .'

'No problem,' said George. 'Could happen to anyone.' He sat down beside her. She sat up now, feeling better. Two girls came towards them. 'Everything OK?' asked one.

'Yeah,' said George. 'Don't worry. Matilda just felt a bit faint.'

'Well, I'm sure you'll be happy to look after her, George,' joked the other girl. And they both walked off.

'You feeling OK now? Do you think you should go back to the hostel? Maybe have a lie-down?'

'No, no way. I don't want people to think I'm a total wimp,' said Matilda.

George didn't seem to think it odd that she had fainted. He must assume it was because she hadn't eaten, or because of the sun. But she knew it was more than that. She looked over towards the house again. The man with the long hair had gone, along with his followers.

What was the shadow that had rushed towards her? It must have been a cloud going across the sun. She looked at the sky. It was the blue of a children's picture book. There was not a cloud in sight.

B is for blue balloon blowing above beautiful blueberry bushes.

'So,' she said after a few moments, as she stood up carefully, with George helping her. 'Who was Gemma?'

'Gemma?'

'The girl. You were going to tell me something. What happened?'

'I don't know what you're talking about,' said George, looking away.

Matilda looked round. Was someone coming? No, she could just see the others, still picking fruit, out of earshot.

'We should get back to work,' said George. 'You get paid for what you pick and I don't know about you, but I can't afford to lose money.'

Matilda didn't repeat her question. She resumed working and they gradually moved further apart. People mostly worked quietly and quickly, she noticed. Every now and then you'd find yourself passing someone else on the other side of the row and you'd exchange a few comments. She learned a few more names like that. People seemed friendly but didn't ask too many questions. There was an air of acceptance, as though anyone could be anyone and no one would notice, or care, or judge. You could dress how you wanted, say what you wanted, think what you wanted. No one would tell you what to be. There was no edge to this world. It was almost frightening. There were too many paths. And no signposts at all. Put a small child in a sweet shop and he doesn't know where to start choosing.

Once when she'd been small, she'd rescued a bird with a damaged wing. She'd kept it safe in a box, fed it worms and caterpillars and dead flies she'd collected from window sills. And when it was better, she'd opened the box and gently tipped the bird out. The bird hopped around a bit and went straight back in the box. It died three days later.

It probably couldn't face the endless freedom, she thought.

George didn't come close enough for her to speak to him again. But she sensed he wasn't going to tell her, anyway. Not yet. He had seemed almost frightened.

Every now and then one or two of the strange people from the big house would walk through the field, perhaps commenting to one of the workers, or asking a question. Rachel came by once and asked Matilda how she was doing. 'Fine, thank you,' Matilda replied, as keen as the others seemed to please her employers. Why did she feel like that? She'd never been one for automatically obeying authority before. But there was something strangely calming about these people, always meeting her gaze as though looking inside her. Their eyes were almost magnetic.

As Rachel walked away, she left behind a very odd calm.

But when Rachel was out of sight, Matilda felt less comfortable. Questions began to form inside her. Who were they? What was special about them? Why did they all live in the big house and what did they do there?

In her mind, she began to call them the Beautiful People. Because they all were. Clean and apple-healthy and poplar-straight. Their faces were all strong, their skin clear. You could imagine them washing in the dew on midsummer's morning. Eating watermelon for breakfast. Drinking chamomile tea. Or more likely peppermint – that would be fresher, clearer. Bread would be home-made, wholemeal. They wouldn't eat meat. She knew the type.

The sun was lasering down now. Matilda had stopped several times to put sun cream on, and was careful to keep drinking water. But she was hungry, and very glad when at midday a whistle blew and someone shouted, 'Lunchtime!'

Matilda followed the others towards a small tractor that was swaying its way towards them. One of the Beautiful People handed down some boxes full of filled rolls. Apples. Even some strawberries. They all sat in the shade of some trees between the fields, and ate and drank and chatted. There were people from different countries. South Africa, Australia, Germany, Denmark. The different voices washed over her and she was happy to listen. She could see Cally and Jack in other groups further away across the fields. George came and sat down next to Matilda. 'OK?'

'Yeah, apart from the green fingers and the scratches and the aching shoulders.'

'It gets worse.' He grinned.

And it did. The half-hour break for lunch meant that when she started picking again her muscles had seized up. By the time the shift was over at three o'clock and they were sitting in the trucks to take them back to the hostel, Matilda was exhausted.

Not too tired to make sure that she was sitting next to Matt, though. 'Hi,' she said. Matt didn't notice. 'Hi,' she said, more loudly.

He turned to her. Took his headphones out of his ears. She noticed it was the latest, most expensive MP3 player. Even better than the one she had left at home because her parents said she'd be mad to take it with her. 'Never know what sort of people you're going to meet on this fruit farm,' her father had said.

'Hi,' she repeated. 'I'm Matilda. I just started today.'

'That's a coincidence.' He was smiling right at her.

'Oh, what?' she asked.

'I'm Matt.'

'Oh! Really!' she exclaimed. 'That's amazing.'

'Where are you from?'

'Edinburgh.'

'London.'

'Hi, Matt from London.'

'Hi, Matilda from Edinburgh.'

And it was amazing how something so complicated could start in such a simple way.

'What you listening to?'

'REM. "Losing My Religion".'

'Cool. My favourite.'

'You wanta listen?'

Matilda leaned back against the rattling truck, sharing the headphones with Matt from London. His shoulder against hers was the best feeling she had had all day.

It was enough to drive the shadow away.

# 5

## S is for Sweet Smoke
## and Suspicion

That evening, Matilda, Jack and Cally sat eating a bean stew in the dining-room. They'd spent the afternoon doing various jobs around the farm. Matilda had helped in the shop for a while. Jack and Cally had weighed and packed strawberries. By the time the evening meal came, they knew their way around everywhere and several names were now familiar.

The Beautiful People came and went. You didn't know they were there and then when you least expected them, or least needed them, suddenly there they were, drifting past on a waft of calmness.

'What do you think of the people who live in the house?' she asked Cally and Jack as they finished the surprisingly good stew.

'They seem nice,' said Cally. 'You know, friendly. Seem to want to make sure we were OK.'

'Yeah,' agreed Jack, leaning his tall frame back in his chair. 'They don't do much work, but looks like they run the place well. In a kind of old-fashioned way. I'd thought it would be much more high-tech. You know, conveyor belts and stuff.'

'But don't you think they seem weird?' Matilda lowered her voice, remembering what George had said.

'No, not really,' said Jack.

'Cally? Come on, they are. Weird.'

'Not really, no,' said Cally. 'I just think the whole place feels really nice, you know, calm? They seem to care. My dad was giving me all these warnings about exploitation and slave-driving, but this seems fine. Her hair was golden, already, streaked even blonder from one day in the sun. Jack reached to flick an eyelash from her cheek and suddenly leaned to kiss her, his dark hair flopping over his face. Couldn't they leave each other alone for a minute?

'Well, I think they're weird. Anyway, what're you guys doing this evening?' If they weren't going to agree with her, she wanted to change the subject.

'We thought we'd hang out in the TV-room. Then get an early night. We're bushed, aren't we, Jack?' said Cally, holding his hand, their fingers linked like two combs stuck together.

'Matilda probably is too. Gooseberry bushed!' Jack grinned at Matilda.

'Oh, come on, let's *do* something!' she said, ignoring

his teasing. 'Come on, it's our first night away from home – well, apart from last night. We should be *doing* something.'

'What? Like hitting the town? Exactly what town would that be? The nearest place with anything interesting going on is probably Dartmoor prison. Come and watch TV with us. Meet some people.'

Matilda followed them out of the dining-room and envied their closeness. How long did it take to get that far? Could that happen one day to her? Her and Matt? And where was Matt, anyway? She hadn't seen him at the meal. And she had looked. 'Want to play cards?' someone called. God! TV or cards. Some choice. If she'd been back at home, she'd have had bars and clubs to consider. Or least, once she'd dealt with the worried nagging of her parents.

She thought of phoning them, thought she should. No point in them being crosser with her than necessary. Besides, there was something oddly reassuring about the idea of speaking to them. She opened her phone. No signal. The hostel was in a dip between hills. She felt cut off. Enjoy it, she tried to tell herself. But it left a whispering feeling of disquiet.

Matilda had never been somewhere where there was nothing to do. Nothing laid on. She didn't have any of the usual things that made her life comfortable and easy.

The TV in her own bedroom, the Internet, the telephone, money, taxis, her own en suite bathroom. It wasn't easy to have nothing when you were used to everything.

'I'm going outside,' she said to the others when they got to the TV-room door. She had looked in and seen a few people sitting around playing cards, others silently watching some loud programme which she would never have chosen to watch.

She went out of the front door.

The evening air was still heavy with the day's heat. Thick and buzzing. Midges flew around her face as she stood in the light of the doorway. She brushed them away, a feeling of irritation creeping over her. She walked away from the lights of the building, towards some trees.

She stopped. Listened. Heard a cough. Looked into the grey darkness. A tiny moving light almost at ground level. The crack of a twig. Cautiously, she walked towards whoever it was.

She knew who it was before he called her name.

'Hi, Matt. What're you doing out here?'

A sweet smoke smell, like burning apricots. Whatever he'd been smoking, he wasn't now. He held nothing in his hands. She could see the weak curl of smoke coming from the ground near where he sat.

'I like it out here,' he said. 'I like being on my own.'

'Oh, sorry. I'll be going then.'

'No, not you.' And she melted. 'It's just they sit there in front of the TV every night and God knows what they're watching. I come out here with my music and sometimes someone joins me and sometimes someone doesn't. And sometimes we have something to drink, and sometimes we don't.'

'And sometimes you smoke something and sometimes you don't?'

He probably smiled but she couldn't see in the near-dark.

'Come and join me? Just to sit, I mean. Oh, and I've got some strawberries.'

'Oh well, then, in that case. Anything except gooseberries.'

She sat down next to him and remembered his smell from when their shoulders had touched before. Clean but not too clean.

'OK, Matilda from Edinburgh. Why are you so far from home? Don't they have fruit farms in Scotland?'

'Yeah, they do. It's a dangerous country to pick fruit in, though.'

'Oh?'

'Wild haggises. Everywhere. They leap out and give you a nasty bite, just when you least expect it.'

'I never knew that. You are an education to me, Matilda from Edinburgh.'

And so the conversation went, easy, almost as though she'd known him for ever. But it didn't feel like that at all, not when she thought about it. It felt brand new and dizzying and breathless. She was aware of the air on her skin, the precise space she occupied, the feeling that every breath she took, every word she spoke, changed the world for ever.

Then he lit up his smoke again. 'Do you mind?' he asked. And a loosening feeling ran through her, as though she was on the verge of something.

'Can I have a smoke? A drag,' she asked, as if this was something she did.

'Nope. It's bad for you.'

'How come you get to do it then?'

'I'm damaged already. I'm a lost cause.'

'Hey, do you want me to beg? I left home yesterday. I want to do this. Once won't hurt.'

'Nah. You're too beautiful. You should look after yourself. Trust me.'

' "Trust me, I'm a pothead." Is that what you're saying?'

'Trust me, you're beautiful. You can kiss me but you can't smoke my weed.'

For a long, diving moment she said nothing, let the

dangerous idea wash around her head, let the taste of it envelop her, let it draw her down into itself. In another time or another place, even yesterday, she might have spoken, or let in a cautious thought, told herself to be careful, play it cool, not give herself away with such abandon. But she closed her mind to the rule of reason and went with her guts and her heart. She would live for now. Nothing else mattered.

And she hardly breathed as she kissed him and the sweet smoke drifted up her nose and into her head. As her hand went to the back of his neck and his hands both crept round her back, her body folded into his and she felt every part of him strong against her.

His tongue was soft on hers and his hands firm and when they broke away she felt weak. Breathless, and with a slight sweat all over her.

She could sense him smile. 'Well, Matilda from Edinburgh. I guess this could be a good summer. Strawberry?'

She took one.

'So, what do you think of the Lilies?' he said after a while.

'The what?'

'The Lilies. It's what I call the weirdos in white shirts. The bosses.'

'Why Lilies?'

'Consider the lilies? You know in the Bible? It says something about, "Consider the lilies – they do sod all work and yet they get everything they need. Theirs is the Kingdom of Heaven." That's what I call the house on the hill – Heaven.'

'Does it say "sod all" in the Bible?'

'Don't know. It's a while since I read it. But that was the gist of it. I kind of worked out that it meant, "Be a lazy bastard and, as long as you look good, God will provide." It's an interesting theory. One I'm trying to live by. I can't say God has provided much as far as I am concerned, though.'

'Why? What's the problem?'

'Oh, nothing for you to worry about. Just I'm not exactly a big success story. Things I touch tend to fall apart. Kind of as though there's someone watching me and as soon as things start to go right that someone just leaps out and casts a bloody great shadow over everything.'

Matilda shivered. It was his voice. Sort of weighed down, suddenly.

'Hey, let's get you inside,' said Matt. He helped her up and they walked out of the trees and into the lights of the hostel, talking easily.

'They're religious, of course, the Lilies,' he said as they approached the hostel. 'Nothing wrong with that, but they're way over the top with it. Wacky. More than wacky. I've discovered some things about them, actually.'

'Go on.'

But they were too near the hostel now. 'Not now. It'll take too long. Tomorrow evening. Same time, same place?'

At the door, she paused. Matt turned towards her and they kissed again. Inside her rolled the softest melting heat and his musky apricot smell sifted through her body like lust. Afterwards, he leaned back and looked straight into her eyes. 'Very nice, Matilda from Edinburgh,' he said, smiling in that dissolving way he had. Then he stopped smiling suddenly. He was looking at something behind her.

She looked around. One of the Lilies. Standing, watching them. As they broke apart, the Lily turned and walked away, without saying anything.

'What's wrong?' asked Matilda.

'I don't know. Just did you see the way she looked at us?' he said quietly. 'God, that lot are weird. Probably think kissing is a sin. Anyway, from the look on her face, you'll be picking gooseberries all summer. And I'll probably be digging potatoes or something, starting from tomorrow. Bang goes what could have been a really beautiful relationship.'

But he couldn't have been too worried because he pulled her to him and kissed her again.

# 6

## D is for Delicious. Danger.

Matt was wrong about one thing. Matilda was put on raspberries the next day. A plum job, she joked. And Rachel gave her an extra-big smile and an extra-warm good morning when she arrived at the shed to be allocated her field.

He was wrong about something else, too. He wasn't made to dig potatoes. He was to pick raspberries with Matilda. They raised their eyebrows at each other. Nothing to worry about, after all. Nothing to spoil the way his smile seemed to slip through her like fingers through water.

The others had already noticed something between them. Jack and Cally grinned at her and waved as they went off to different fields. And as Matilda watched them go, she felt part of something. As though she had an anchor, to stop her floating away into the nowhere sky. As though she had joined a new and better world. She belonged. For once, nothing else, past or future, seemed to matter. No shadows now. Even if she looked behind her, she knew there would be no shadows.

Matilda and Matt walked towards the raspberry canes, shoulders close. They did no more than brush arms. It was enough, for now. But she looked forward to later. She looked forward to the rest of the summer stretching ahead and apple-pie dreams coming true. She spent a happy morning, avoiding the Lilies where possible, knowing, hoping, that Matt was wanting her as much as she wanted him.

Every now and then she stopped to watch his easy body move between the raspberry lines. He was not the same as anyone she had fancied before. He was somehow . . . oddly . . . dangerous. She surprised herself with that thought. Dangerous? How? Maybe because he was older than her, and seemed older than he was, unlike the boys she was used to. He knew what he wanted and took it, smoked weed but didn't want her to, seemed unshakable. Carelessly wise. And yet there was something else about him, something which she saw when he didn't know she was looking at him. Something like sadness. What was it he had said? That when he touched things they fell apart? That he was damaged? What had he meant?

Why did he seem dangerous? Deliciously dangerous. Why did she instinctively know that her parents would not approve of him? Even if they didn't know about the drugs.

All morning, Matilda felt the distant presence of the house on the hill. Watching them carefully from afar. She would not look at it. 'Heaven,' as Matt called the house. Though with the distinct impression that heaven was not somewhere he aspired to.

Before lunch, a message came for Matt to go back to the hostel. He didn't come back to the raspberry fields.

Matilda never saw Matt alive again.

# 7

## C is for Confusion

Where had he gone? What had happened? Matilda spent the next few hours wondering, going through all the reasons, innocent or otherwise, why he might not have come back. He had been allocated to another job on the farm? He had had a phone call? One of his parents was ill? Someone had died?

As the sun blazed down, her brain became slow. She picked raspberries mechanically, the voices of the other workers nothing more than haze at the edges of her consciousness. Every now and then she found herself staring towards the house on the hill. Heaven. It danced and shimmered in the heat and sometimes the sunlight bounced from the glasshouses like angel arrows, blinding her. Once or twice, she saw groups of people wandering up and down in front of the house, but the raspberry field was further away than where she had been yesterday and it was hard to make out any detail. She did not see the man with the Jesus hair. She wanted to see him and yet was afraid too. She wanted him to be there and for him to raise his arms towards her, and she wanted to see if the shadow ran towards her as before, or if perhaps it had been her imagination. It must have been her imagination. She hoped it was. And yet a growing part of her wanted the mystery, the sense of something inexplicable, something to wonder about.

A cloud going across the sun was altogether too dull an explanation. She wanted more meaning, even if it *was* frightening. Even if it made her faint. She wanted to lose control that way. To dive off the edge and believe someone would catch her. Like kissing Matt.

When the cart brought their lunch, she sat on the edge of the group. George was not in her group today. She was glad. She did not want to speak to him right now. She only wanted to speak to Matt. George would be too sensible, too safe.

Her parents would like George.

Her head began to swim. She was wearing a baseball cap and it was too tight. Her long hair was protecting the back of her neck from the sun but she could feel the sting at the side of her neck where she had not put enough cream on. If she looked in a mirror, she knew she would see freckles. She pulled up the sleeves of her T-shirt so they were at shoulder level. Better to have a line at shoulder level than part-way down her arms.

She'd need to wear something different tomorrow, to try to get an all-over tan.

She tried to relax, to forget the gad-fly of worry that began to buzz behind her eyes. But she could not help scanning the fields for any sign of Matt coming back.

Fruit-picking finished at three o'clock again and she went straight to find one of the Lilies. There was no one in the hostel. She went towards the café. There was a queue of people, members of the public who had been picking their own strawberries and now wanted lunch. Sweating families suspiciously scanned the organic options on the menu. 'Organic corn-fed chicken goujons with crushed aubergine dip and mango salsa – look, it's just like chicken nuggets,' announced one pink-faced mother to her brat who was wailing for McDonalds. 'And you can leave the dips. And look, they've got ice-cream. For afters, mind.'

The only Lily there was busy behind the counter, a saintly smile on her beautiful face as she quickly processed the dizzying requests from the public and dispensed organic Devon chips and freshly-squeezed Fair-trade orange juice, accompanied by melon-sweet wishes for them to, 'Have a lovely day.'

She was too busy. Matilda could not ask her where Matt was. She turned away. Looked at her watch. She was going to be late for her next job, cleaning the hostel.

'Hello, Matilda!' It was Maggie, the first Lily they had met when they arrived. 'Are you OK? You're looking a bit lost.'

'No, I just . . . well, I wanted to know about Matt.'

'Matt who?'

'I don't know his surname, actually. Just that he was called away this morning and he never came back and I just wondered . . . I mean, is everything OK?'

Maggie's face flickered, though she still smiled. 'Oh, you must mean the boy we had to ask to leave. Matthew. Was he a good friend of yours?'

'Asked to leave? Why?'

'Look, Matilda, you're going to find out about this soon, anyway. I am sorry if Matt was a friend of yours but I am afraid we had to ask him to leave. The rules of our farm are quite clear and drugs simply are not allowed. Yes, I am afraid that we found drugs amongst Matt's things and when we questioned him he admitted that they were his. We could have called the police, but we didn't. I think he was grateful for that. I have to say – and do keep this to yourself, Matilda, for your friend's sake – but I have to say that this was not the first time. He did admit that he had a record and really couldn't afford to be arrested again. He promised to leave immediately if we didn't report him.'

'But . . . did he leave a message at all? For me?'

'No, Matilda, I don't believe he did. I think he was just glad to get away without police involvement, to be honest.'

'What about his phone number? I want to contact him. We'd only just met and . . .' She stopped, her hopes of a beautiful summer falling away into nothing.

Maggie stepped closer, put her arm round Matilda's shoulders and guided her towards the hostel. She smelled sweet, clean, like strawberries. But − Christ! − everything smelled of sodding strawberries around here.

'Poor Matilda. I am so sorry. But, you know, you're better off finding this out now. I mean, you wouldn't want to get too close to someone like that, would you?'

'Someone like what?' asked Matilda. 'Just because he smoked hash. What harm does that do to anyone else? He was kind, nice, honest. I liked him.'

'There are things you don't know, Matilda,' said Maggie. 'I think Matt was not quite as he seemed. Obviously, I can't tell you everything, but trust me, you are better moving on and forgetting about him. There are lots of other lovely people here, and you've got your whole life ahead of you. We'll look after you, Matilda, really we will.' She stopped, looked deeply at her. Matilda felt her eyes prickle with silly tears. Maggie smiled. 'Here, come on, let me give you a hug.' And she pulled her close. For a moment, Matilda held back, but then she realised that the warmth that came from this girl not much older than herself was like a blanket. She wanted to be rolled up in it. She felt herself relax and a strange calm flow over her.

A sudden noise of an accelerating engine shot her back to reality. Both of them turned. A car was scrunching through the gravel of the car park too fast and screeching to a halt, sliding into a stone bollard with an ugly smashing of metal. Matilda could see the driver's face as it happened. It was David, his jaw set rigidly.

Maggie ran towards him. Matilda followed.

David was getting out of the car when Maggie and Matilda arrived. He was unhurt, though looking dazed.

'David! Are you all right?'

'Yeah, I'm fine. Don't know how that happened.' He quickly went round to the front of the car. The bumper was distorted, almost broken in half, and hanging off. 'Well, bang goes my no claim bonus,' he said, smiling his gorgeous smile once more. 'Hi, Matilda. Sorry about that. Doesn't do much for my street cred, does it?'

Maggie turned to her. 'Matilda, you'd better get back to whatever you're supposed to be doing now. And, hey, remember what I said. Move forward and we'll all look after you.' And she smiled, but it was a distracted, distant smile. Fragile as a petal.

Matilda went up towards the hostel, her feelings

confused. She wanted to see Matt. And then she realised she knew nothing about him at all. Where did he live? She didn't even know his surname. Didn't have his mobile phone number. And maybe there *were* things about him that she would not want to know.

Maybe he should join the shadows. Maybe she should just look ahead into the light, move forward as Maggie had said.

And yet she ached for Matt.

Maggie obviously knew more about Matt than she did. Yet Matt had also said he had discovered some things about them. What should she believe? How did you know what was the truth?

Maggie and David seemed to care about her.

So had Matt. In his dangerous, dreamy way. His damaged way. Everything he touched fell to pieces, he'd said. Maybe she would have fallen to pieces if he'd stayed. And maybe she'd have enjoyed falling to pieces.

She felt close to tears again. She wanted him. She'd only met him one day ago. Why did it have to end so quickly? He made her feel . . . everything. Hot. Alive.

But how could he have left without leaving her a message?

Had she been deceived? It was completely possible that he had not cared at all. That she was just some girl who had come to him while he was stoned and who

73

immediately let herself be kissed and who seemed to want even more.

Well, that much was true, wasn't it? She did want more. So what? This was freedom. She could use it how she wanted. It wasn't as though she'd ever planned to be a nun.

Matilda finished her cleaning tasks in a daze. Her thoughts circled each other. He cared. He didn't care. He cared. He didn't care.

She cared. Didn't she? She wanted him and he had been snatched away from her. Why did he have to be so stupid and so careless? Why couldn't she have what she wanted? Why did freedom have to be so damned difficult?

# 8

## L is for Losing

'Shit, shit and triple shit,' muttered Matt, as he walked slowly along the narrow road, the hedges high and enclosing. His rucksack was heavy on his back, the straps digging into his shoulders and the sweat sticking his hair to his forehead. But worse than that was the knowledge that he had failed. Again. 'Shit.'

Why? Why sack him so suddenly? Without warning. They knew he smoked hash sometimes. They'd never shown much interest before. Yes, so there were clear rules. But he never did it indoors. Or while working. He was discreet. And he never dealt. For Christ's sake, he didn't even let Matilda smoke any because he knew the truth. That hash had fucked him up. That's why he carried on taking it. Too late to stop. Too fucked up. He needed it to plug the holes in his head. But he wasn't far enough gone to let someone else go down the same dead-end lane. Not someone as cute as Matilda.

Christ, why did he have to fancy her? If he hadn't been in a fug of don't-give-a-shit at that particular moment, he probably would've controlled himself better. Then the Lily wouldn't have seen them kiss. Because he knew fine why she, the Lily, had stared at him like that. Because until Matilda had come along, he had been sucking up to that particular Lily. He'd been playing on her sympathies, telling her how he didn't have any friends, didn't know how to get along with people, hard childhood, abusive parents, that sort of crap. She was going to be his way of getting into Heaven. The house on the hill. So he could investigate what was going on there. He knew something about religious groups, how they home in on vulnerable people and suck them in. And seeing him kissing another girl, well, that kind of wrecked his image as a vulnerable social outcast, didn't it? Was that why he was chucked out? Nothing to do with drugs?

Shit, shit and triple shit.

How was he going to explain this? This was going to be his big chance to prove himself. His final chance. And it had been going well. He had already discovered some interesting information, after just a couple of weeks. Still didn't know what was going on but there was definitely something. Something sinister. And if he'd only been able to stay a while longer he knew he could have got into the house. Infiltrated the weird cult he knew in his guts was up there. And wouldn't that have been the scoop of the year? A dead-cert way of promotion to a permanent position. He had been so sure of himself, so sure this was a seriously dangerous cult, that he had been careful not to tell anyone where it was based. He didn't want any of the other reporters getting in on the act.

He had to get back there. He couldn't just allow them to chuck him out. The creepy bastards with their perfect smiles.

And what about Matilda? She *was* cute. But it was never going to be anything serious. Just a boy and a girl and a few sex hormones. It wasn't her fault that he had been chucked out but if it hadn't been for her being there . . . No, it *was* his fault. He had to admit that. And if his suspicions were correct, surely she was in danger now? And even if she had been just a bit of fun, fuelled by some weed and hormones on a careless summer's evening, he didn't want to harm her, did he?

He didn't even have her phone number. She didn't have his. Christ, they didn't even know each other's surname. He needed to be able to warn her. He had left a note, written in a hurry and probably not explaining himself clearly – but would she even find it? He had been watched carefully as he packed. The only time he'd been alone was in the toilets. The chances of Matilda guessing that that was the only place he could have put a note were remote. Very remote. Even if she guessed he'd written a note in the first place. More likely she'd think he was just some pothead who had dumped her and didn't care about her at all. Well, maybe he was a pothead, but he was a decent one, wasn't he? Somehow, he must get back there.

He must do something right. Prove everyone wrong. Everyone, ever since he could remember, had assumed he would cock up. And usually he had. Not just usually. Always, to be honest. Every time he tried to succeed, to turn it all around, something would go wrong. But this time would be different.

He stopped. Turned round. Looked back up the road, squinting into the pounding sun. A car was coming towards him. Fast. He stood at the side of the road as it approached. He couldn't even see what colour it was in the glare. He could see it shimmering in the heat. He could hear it now.

Too fast for such a narrow country road.

He wanted to make some sort of sign for it to slow down. A shudder of strange fear rushed through him. The car seemed to be coming straight at him. He wanted to step further back from the road, but these sodding Devon lanes were impossible. No verges. Thick hedges higher than his head. No room to move.

Christ, it *was* coming straight at him.

He gasped as he felt the wind. Felt pain on his leg as a stone flew up and hit him.

And then the car was past. The road was empty again. Gradually, his heart stopped pounding.

The treacle sun was melting his brain. He couldn't think. What should he do? Go back? Go back and warn Matilda? Get her away from there? But he'd be spotted. And how would he get her away? Or should he walk to the next town – wherever the hell that was – find somewhere to stay, hire a car, and work out what to do and how to contact Matilda? Maybe even get her to help him with his investigation.

That would probably be more sensible. But he probably didn't have enough money to stay somewhere, or for a car. No, he must go back to the farm. He would sleep rough in the nearby fields, or a farm shed or whatever, be near the fruit farm so that he could do something as quickly as possible. So that he could act and make everything right.

How far from the farm was he? He'd been walking more than an hour, and then he'd hitched a lift in a van for about twenty minutes. Probably about twenty miles altogether.

He felt a sudden sense of urgency. He needed to warn Matilda now. The more he thought, the more it seemed obvious that she'd never find the note.

He needed a smoke. But no, that was what had caused this – if he hadn't been so relaxed last night, he wouldn't have kissed Matilda in public, and the Lily wouldn't have seen. Christ, maybe it wasn't even that – maybe the Lily had heard him talking to Matilda. Didn't he say something about knowing some things about them? He went cold. They couldn't have heard, could they? Was it just then that the Lily had looked at him so weirdly?

He had to get back there.

He turned again and started to walk fast towards the fruit farm. He put his headphones in his ears and switched his MP3 player on, letting the music surround him. Even with his shades, he squinted in the searing sun. As he walked, sweating, he planned what he would do. How he would complete this assignment, turn his life around, make something of himself. Maybe even give up the hash. Maybe. Easy to say.

The music beat into his head. 'Losing my Religion.' His favourite track. 'Life is bigger. It's bigger than you.'

He never heard the other sounds of life around him. Never heard the scream of death spinning down the road behind him. Never saw the dust and shimmer and the blazing eyes of the car. Never even felt . . .

> Life is bigger
> It's bigger than you
> And you are not me

# 9

## S is for Silence in
## Strawberry Fields

When Matilda had finished her chores that afternoon, her hands tight and uncomfortably dry from the dust and water of a couple of hours' housework, she went outside with a mug of tea. The fields were nearly empty. All the picking of the day went on before three o'clock, apart from the pick-your-own customers, dilatory trails of families drooping in the wilting heat.

In the distance, on another hill, stood Heaven. She ached with a hungry emptiness as she thought of Matt. She wished he could be there next to her and she could feel his heat and what he did to her insides.

What had he been going to tell her? He had said he had discovered something. So had George. Maybe George could tell her.

'Hey, Matty. How you doing?' It was Cally. Beneath her sun-streaked hair, her cheekbones and nose were a sweet toffee-pink. Her long legs were just the sort of legs every girl wanted. Cally maybe didn't have the comfortable money that Matilda's family had but her life was easy in other ways. Still, Matilda could forgive her. She was her best friend, after all. Always had been, ever since she could remember. Cally had helped her through . . . everything. Cally understood. Even the feeling of Cally beside her now was comforting. Cally would always say the right thing, and be honest, too.

Matilda told her about Matt. 'And now he's gone, Cally, and God, yeah, I mean I'd only known him less than two days, but I really fancied him.'

'I'm really sorry, Matty. But he broke the rules, I suppose. I mean, everyone knows the rules. Those notices everywhere. And hey, there's more fish, as they say.'

'It's all right for you. You've got Jack. You'll probably end up getting married to Jack and I'll still be flinging myself at all the wrong people and getting hurt.'

Cally said nothing. They stood for a moment, drinking their tea. Matilda began to feel the shadow creeping up on her again. It was still behind her but she could sense its presence, almost hear it slithering across the ground towards her feet. She knew if she wasn't careful the tears would squeeze from her eyes. God, how she wished she could scream at the shadow to go away, to piss off out of her life and go and stalk someone else. But depression wasn't like that, she knew. If she *could* have shouted at it, it would have gone, but depression steals your voice. You need all your breath for breathing and there's none left for shouting at shadows. Sometimes you just have to curl up and wait for them to pass.

Yet, sometimes those shadows are the blanket you want.

S is for shadows softly sliding.

Silence. Smother. Suffer.

And surrender.

No! She would not let it come this time. She forced a smile onto her face. Hey, *Matty*, she thought, *you're just feeling sorry for yourself! Snap out of it*.

Footsteps. They both turned. Jack. His tall gangly body loped towards them, thumbs hooked into his pockets. Even Jack's face, normally pale under his dark hair, had a sun-tinged pink to it.

'Hi there, you two. Can I join you?' He looked at Cally. She looked uncomfortable.

'Hey, Jack. How was your day?' asked Matilda, determined to stay in the sunshine.

'Not bad. You?' His face looked concerned. She presumed he'd heard about Matt being sacked. She soon discovered that was not why he was looking concerned. Before waiting for her answer, he turned to Cally. 'You told her?' His voice quiet, stupidly, because it was nowhere near quiet enough. It was the sort of voice that says, 'If I say this quietly perhaps it won't be so bad.'

'No, not yet. I was just about to, but . . .'

'What?' Matilda looked from one to the other. What was going on?

'Not a good time, Jack,' said Cally.

'Oh, right, oops,' he said, going red. There was a leaf in his hair. A scratch on his cheek. Sunburn on the tops of his ears. Ordinary things. Jack was an ordinary guy. That was what was great about him. He had no side. No itchy edge.

'What?' Matilda demanded again. 'Come on, you have to say. For Christ's sake, tell me!'

Cally linked her arm into Matilda's. She gestured to Jack to go away and he did. 'The thing is, Matty, something's turned up. You remember that job Jack applied for in that PR agency and didn't hear about? Turns out there was some cock-up and someone was off sick and they thought they'd contacted him. And he did get it! He just got a message from his mum. So we're both going.' She began to speak more quickly, seeing Matilda's sunken face. 'But listen, Matty, come with us. It'll be cool. We're going to rent a flat and there'll be room – you can sleep on the floor or something. Hey, it'll be so great. Just think, our own flat! Forget the fruit-picking – you know it wasn't what we really wanted.

And you and I can easily get jobs in London, you know, waitressing or something. Come with us, Matty.'

But the fruit-picking *was* what Matilda wanted. It was what she had dreamed about and planned. It was all part of her ideal summer. It was all tied up with freedom. The three of them had talked about it for months. She felt like a child without a promised birthday party.

The right words were stuck somewhere. Tangled up. She said nothing. Could say nothing.

'Matty? Hey, come on. Please come with us.' There was a note of desperation in Cally's voice now. But Matilda knew it wasn't because Cally couldn't bear to leave her friend. It was because Cally couldn't bear to feel guilty. Because feeling guilty wasn't part of feeling perfect. Of course they wouldn't really want her sleeping on the floor of their flat. A gooseberry for the whole summer?

'When are you going?' Her voice surprised her with its flatness.

'Well, I don't know. Soon. As soon as we can organise it. Probably work till the end of the week, get a week's wages, at least. Depends. But you'll come, won't you?'

'No. Of course I won't bloody come. You can't just snap your fingers and expect me to do just what you and

Jack want, you know. I *have* got a life of my own.' Her voice was brittle and she struggled to control it.

Cally said nothing now. She opened her mouth but nothing came out. She put her hand out towards Matilda, perhaps to touch her arm, anything.

Matilda started to walk away. 'See you later. I assume you'll say goodbye before you go?'

'Don't be unfair, Matilda,' said Cally, angry now. 'Christ, don't be so spoilt. Why do you always have to manipulate people? You can't stop everyone else being happy, you know, just because you won't let yourself be. You dream and then, when your dreams don't come true, you blame everyone else. Well, don't sodding dream so much, then.'

But Matilda was walking away and would not let Cally see her face. She walked towards the strawberry fields and breathed and breathed and breathed until the fury sank into something more comfortably like sadness. She could hear Cally shouting after her. Cally would be feeling sorry that she had hurt her. Let her be sorry.

Matilda walked towards the house on the hill. Everything was sliding away, slipping through her fingers. At the edge of the strawberry field, she stopped. Tried to open her head to the sounds around her. To feel the breeze on her face and smell the straw below her feet. Breathe in the sunlight. But she felt nothing.

She sat down. Lay flat on the ground and stared up into the ocean above her. The world swirled around her head. She felt like a speck spinning down into a whirlpool, powerless and alone.

How do you fight the shadows? If there's light, the shadows inevitably follow. Don't they? Isn't that the whole point about light? Without light, there's no shadow.

Suddenly she needed to call home. It was something reliable. She took her phone out of her pocket. Switched it on. There was a signal out here. She had four missed calls and eight text messages. Five of the text messages were from friends. Friends with other jobs and holidays and plans. She blinked back tears as she smiled through their careless, unknowing words, words which reached uselessly out to her like a sleepwalker's smile. The other texts and all the missed calls were from her parents.

'Hello m. Is all well? Contact us soon. Love, mx

'Dear Matilda, we need to know if all well. Dad x'

'Worried. Phone or text. Please. SOON. Mxx'

She pressed the buttons and listened to the phone ringing in her house. Imagined them looking at each other. 'There's the phone, dear,' her father would be saying. But her mother would be halfway to it before the first ring had settled in her ears.

'Eight seven two four.' Her mother.

'Hello, it's me.'

'Matilda, why didn't you phone? We've been so worried.'

'Sorry. I tried but there's no signal down where the hostel is and we're not allowed to take mobiles out to the fields,' she lied.

'Anyway, sweetheart, how are you? Meeting nice people? Are they feeding you properly? What's the weather like?'

'Everything's fine. The people are nice.'

'How are Cally and Jack?'

Hesitation. 'Fine.'

'And how many other people are working there? How big is the farm? And have you got a suntan? Oh, it's so lovely to speak to you, Matilda.' Her mother's bright voice crackled at the edges, emotion spilling over in her excitement. Catch her off guard and her mother had sparkle. Catch her without her shield, and something unfamiliar glinted inside. A pilot light of life. A half-forgotten warmth and a memory of how to live.

'I . . .'

'Hello, darling.' It was her father coming on the extension. 'Why didn't you phone? We were worried.'

'I've just explained to Mum.'

'We need to hear from you, Matilda. You should

90

have phoned. It's only because we worry.' A clawing twist of a fist inside her stomach. The wrench of irritation.

'Dad's right, sweetheart. It's only because we worry.'

She was silent. Let them fill the silence.

Her mother. 'Anyway, you were saying. About the farm. What have you picked?'

'Fruit.'

Seaweed emotions tangled across the miles.

She finished the conversation as soon as she could. Afterwards, she felt worse. The weather and the fruit and had she met any nice people? Was she eating her greens? Christ, there was more to everything than that. The truth. That she was lonely and frightened. That the shadows were chasing her even here. That she had loved and lost. That everything was falling apart already. That she wanted to come home and yet home was the last place she wanted to go. Because home was what she was escaping from. Or not home, but what was there. The shadow that was over all of them.

But where was she escaping to? A place somehow without shadows. The light in all directions. The noonday sun. Apricot warmth. Somewhere sweet and soft and healing. Was that something you could only dream about?

She looked up to the house on the hill. Heaven.

# 10

## G is for Greenhouses
## And God's Gift

It rained the day Cally and Jack left. The clouds had rolled over the farm the evening before and, in the early hours of the morning, the cold air clutched everything in its dampness. Through the windows they saw the rods of rain, heard them smashing on the wooden roof over the dining area, and knew there would be no fruit-picking that morning. A new rota would be made up and, in the meantime, workers could have some free time. Matilda would rather start working as early as usual, wanted just to get on with it, make the parting quick.

'Come with us,' Cally had pleaded even at the last minute as they stood awkwardly by the door, making conversation, trying to fill the last moments with ordinary things. Matilda shook her head. She wanted to say, 'Stay with me,' but she would not beg. She hugged them both and the three of them hugged together. This was the hardest goodbye Matilda had ever done. Her powerlessness was crushing. The sense of life running away from her. Of everyone knowing what they wanted and finding it, except her.

As her friends hurried down the path towards the car and then drove away, Matilda had never felt more alone. Beyond crying, just sunk and heavy. She wanted to give in to it, to let the rain wash through her and mirror her mood. She stood there for a while, numbed. She wanted someone to come and take her away, someone who cared. Cally. Jack. Matt. Even her parents. Someone to notice what she was feeling.

As she turned back into the hostel, she heard someone call her name. Maggie was hurrying towards her, half hidden by a white kagoule.

'Good morning, Matilda. Are you OK? No, you're not OK, are you? Oh, poor Matilda, your friends have gone, haven't they? You aren't having a great time of it just now, are you?' And she smiled and put her arms round Matilda's shoulders as she guided her into the hostel. 'You need to take your mind off it, you know. Well, if you have a look at today's rota, I think you'll be a little happier.' Maggie put the piece of plastic-sheathed paper in Matilda's hand. She scanned the names. Hers wasn't there.

'I don't see my name,' she said, wiping a drip of rain

off the end of her nose and pushing back her hood.

'No,' said Maggie. 'I thought that's what you'd be pleased about.'

'A day off?' asked Matilda, with a sinking feeling. Why would anyone want a day off when it was pouring with rain, damply cold, and there was nothing to do within thirty miles? This was not exactly a buzzing metropolis with cinemas and shopping malls. Not exactly the centre of the universe.

'No.' Maggie smiled. 'Who'd want a day off on a day like this? You're going somewhere where we don't have rotas.'

Matilda looked at her, not understanding.

'The greenhouses. By the big house. You'll have seen it on the hill.'

H is for Heaven.

Heaven and happiness in a house high on a hill.

Maggie continued, watching Matilda's face. 'Yes, we need some help up there. It's lovely in the greenhouses. Warm, tropical, even if the rain's pouring down outside. I thought you might like something to cheer you up. You've had it a bit rough, what with your friend Matt going and now your other friends. Thought you might be a bit lonely, so I've put you with me this afternoon.'

'Thanks, Maggie. That's really nice of you.' And it

was. Matilda thought there was nothing she would rather do than spend the afternoon up there. Not necessarily with Maggie, but up there in the greenhouses in the warmth. Away from everyone else. In Heaven. She grinned inside as she thought of it. Wished she could tell Matt.

'Great. It'll be OK, you know, Matilda. It will if you want it enough. You can do anything if you want it enough. Because we'll help you. Whatever sadness you have, we can make it go away. It's what we do.'

We.

Maggie's eyes never wavered from Matilda's. Matilda tried to look somewhere else – it felt odd staring at someone's eyes. Normally, you look at other parts of people's faces, maybe glance over their eyes every now and then, but look away as well. But Maggie looked directly at her and soon Matilda found herself doing the same, as though she was pulled.

'Thanks, Maggie,' she said again. 'I appreciate it. Where do I go, and when?'

'Just wait till I've finished a few things here and then I'll drive you up.'

Maggie went off and Matilda waited just inside the entrance to the hostel.

'Hi, Matilda.' She turned. It was George. He looked at her. 'You OK?' Why, what did her face look like?

'Yeah, sure.' She felt oddly embarrassed. As though she'd betrayed him by talking to Maggie. Instinctively, she knew she didn't want him to know.

'Wonder what we'll be doing today?' he said, looking out through the open door at the dolphin-grey sky.

'Yeah,' she said, non-committally.

'Last time it rained, I had to clean all the packing equipment in the barns. Boring.'

'Right. Well, I don't really know what to expect, I suppose.' She wished he would move on, go and do whatever he was going to do.

'You had breakfast?' he asked.

'Yeah. Better go and clean my teeth and stuff, I guess. See you later,' and she began to walk towards her dormitory. Just then, Maggie came back.

'OK, Matilda, shall we go?'

'I just remembered I have to clean my teeth. Can you give me a minute? Sorry,' and she rushed off. She could see George look at her strangely but there was nothing she could do.

She'd already cleaned her teeth, of course. She waited a minute and then hurried back to the front of the building, wiping her mouth. George was standing by the noticeboard.

'See you later,' she said. He said nothing.

As she walked with Maggie down to the car park, she

97

did not look back but she felt George looking at her. Don't be silly, she thought. You can't possibly feel him watching you.

The rain had almost stopped and the sky was lightening to a translucent grey in the east. Matilda hoped it wouldn't improve too much. She was fascinated by the idea of spending time near the house on the hill.

Maggie spoke, as if reading her thoughts. 'Looks as though it'll clear up. Never mind, we'd still like your help in the greenhouses.'

In the car, Matilda settled back and enjoyed the short drive around the road and up the hill from the other side, along little more than a potholed lane. As they crunched up the long gravel drive, the house loomed quickly nearer, its imposing Georgian walls rising high into the clouds.

The sun broke through properly at last and the patch of blue began to bloom across the sky. Maggie swung the car round to the back of the house and parked it near a brick archway. They climbed out and Matilda followed her through an arch rambling with honeysuckle.

There were the greenhouses stretching away, three of them, huge, old, in beautiful condition. Ornate metal gables, painted gleaming white, that must have been original. No one would spend that sort of money nowadays on decorating a commercial venture. Matilda didn't know the names for the parts of the roof, but she could see that the pinnacles and turrets and spirals all added to the sense of majesty.

She saw no one else. The house sat silent, its windows blank. She could hear no surrounding sounds other than the crunch of their footsteps. Everything nearby was tidy. Pots of salmon-pink geraniums and spherical bay trees stood in corners and doorways and nooks. In a huge, raised, stone circle, rosemary bushes and mint and other herbs jostled for position, glistening with recent rain as sudden sunlight speared them.

Maggie led her round to the front of the first greenhouse and opened the door, unlocking it with some sort of swipecard. Matilda followed her in.

The tropical heat hurled itself at her, took her breath away. Immediately, she smelled the intense crispness of tomato plants. Remembered it from home, where her mother grew them in her own greenhouse and had taught Matilda to pinch out the sideshoots with a thumb and forefinger. She put her fingers to her nose now, unthinkingly. Almost closed her eyes as she drank in the sweet tomato heat. She felt any tension ease away in the steamy air.

She had grown a tomato plant herself once. Had

watered it and watered it. Had drowned it, probably, because soon there had been a smell of rotting earth and mildewed roots and the plant had died with a few sickly yellow flowers that never turned to fruit. The stem had been thin and wavy from the start, struggling to drink light amongst all her mother's stronger plants. The leaves had turned yellow and then brown. She had cut them off until there were very few left. And then one day her plant had gone – thrown away.

And she couldn't ask who had thrown it away because that was when her brother died. Perhaps a little before, perhaps a little after. Did it make much difference? It was summer and tomatoes swelled and grew in her mother's greenhouse, from tall triffid-like plants that seemed to creak as they grew so fast and bent under their own weight, but not Matilda's plant. Her mother had grown tomatoes as her brother lay dying, but Matilda's plant had shrivelled and withered.

Perhaps it was because Matilda had cared so much. About the plant. But her mother had not, drifting into the greenhouse only occasionally, absent-mindedly watering or feeding or snipping or tying or staking, or sometimes just standing there as though she had forgotten why she was there. But Matilda had thrown herself into nursing that tomato plant, desperately willing it to live. As her mother had done for her son.

Perhaps you shouldn't ever want something too much. Perhaps the gods are angered by your greed.

Maggie was smiling at her. 'It's an amazing smell, isn't it? Breathe it in, Matilda. It's God's gift to you today. Go with your feeling.'

Matilda wanted to cry amongst the red and green and the wet heat and the sweetness and pain. 'It reminds me of home, that's all. Not that we had anything like this, but we did grow tomatoes. The smell is so . . . special. You never smell tomatoes like that in shops.' She almost wanted to tell Maggie the rest of it.

Maggie twisted a tomato from a nearby plant and handed it to Matilda. 'Here. You'll never taste them like that in shops, either.' The skin was an almost translucent orange, somewhere between red and green.

Matilda bit into it and loved the familiar way the thick skin was exactly the right crunchiness and how the sweetness burst across her tongue. A tomato straight from the plant had the best taste in the world, she thought. It still seemed to breathe for a few seconds after its plucking, and if you ate it in those few seconds you captured something of its nature.

There was nothing like a remembered smell for taking you back to an earlier time. And now the smell brought back her brother dying. The relief, the sweetness, the light in the distance.

The sun now sliced through the glass of the greenhouse and the heat became quickly unbearable. She felt the sweat on her forehead, the way her clothes stuck to her. Felt a trickle of ugly moisture running down her spine.

'That's odd,' Maggie said. 'The roof vents and windows should open automatically when the temperature rises.' She went over to a control panel and fiddled with something. Within a few seconds, Matilda heard a whirring sound and watched as panels slid back in the roof and at the top of the walls. Almost immediately, she felt a breeze sift through and the heat sank to a bearable limit.

Maggie came back. 'Something was stuck. It's done it once or twice before. Anyway, now come over here and I'll show you what I'd like you to do.'

Matilda followed Maggie over to some trestle-tables with boxes of seedlings at various stages of growth.

'I'm afraid it's nothing very exciting,' said Maggie. 'Just cleaning. It's important to keep the surfaces and everything clean, stop the build-up of algae and any mildew on the seed-trays and the pots.' She picked up a lidded container. 'Bother. Empty. Sorry, I'll have to go and get some more cleaning soda. I won't be long,' and she disappeared out of the greenhouse.

The door closed behind her.

# 11

## P is for Passionflower and Peach

Matilda looked around. Trestles stood around one edge of the huge glass building, with rows of tiny seedlings, obediently growing, sprouting the same number of leaves as others in the same tray. Below sat shelves with glass jars, tiny paint brushes, white plastic labels, everything neat. Everywhere else, rows and rows of tomato plants of various sizes stood completely still in the tropical sweat. Tomatoes – red, green, golden, large, small, all hanging heavy from the bigger plants, the branches supported by symmetrical trapezes of green twine.

She walked towards the other side. Peering through the steamy glass of a closed door, she could see through to the next greenhouse. She wiped the glass and made a space to look through. Enormous plants snaked around the walls and entwined with each other across the roof, dripping grapes and peaches. It was like a tropical forest, lush and extraordinary and with everything bigger and wetter and brighter than normal. You could almost imagine snakes and dangerous creatures and enormous spiders in there. She was tempted to open the door and walk through, to drink in the heady warmth which she knew must fill the space. But there didn't seem to be a handle and the door, when pushed, stayed firm. She could see the slot for the swipecard which she didn't have. Remarkably hi-tech. But the contents of these greenhouses were valuable, of course. Thousands of pounds' worth of produce. Not that anyone would steal tomato plants, thought Matilda briefly. But maybe there was something more valuable in the other hothouses.

In the distance she could see another greenhouse beyond the second one. It was difficult to make out what was in it, but she thought she could see enormous red flowers. She had never heard of a fruit that had such enormous bright-red flowers. Surely nothing that would normally grow in this country? What could they be?

'Matilda?' Matilda spun round guiltily. It was Maggie. She was smiling. 'You looking at the grapes and peaches? Wonderful, aren't they? Do you want to come through?'

'Sure.'

And Maggie took her swipecard and slid it in and then out of the slot. She pushed the door and it opened. They walked in and Matilda gazed around the jungle.

Gnarled lianas twisted around each other, trailing soft, thick leaves and spiralling ringlets of vines. And even the woody peach tree branches seemed to spin a web with their wizened fingers so that everything massed and jumbled into an impossible puzzle without end. The more you looked into the leaves, the more hidden fruits appeared.

Maggie reached up and picked two peaches. She handed one to Matilda and Matilda held it in her hand. It felt warm, as if alive. And bigger than any peach she had seen since a holiday in South Africa.

'Eat it,' said Maggie. 'Go on. You deserve it. Pure pleasure.'

They both bit into their fruits and Matilda let the juice run down her chin. It was the ripest taste she had ever known, warm and heady and impossibly full in her mouth. The soft, downy skin was barely strong enough to hold the fruit inside, and disintegrated on her tongue.

'Beautiful,' she exclaimed. 'Just beautiful.' Maggie smiled. Bolder now, Matilda pointed towards the greenhouse with the huge red flowers. 'What's growing in there?'

'Oh, it's just some flowers – a type of passionflower, you know?' She started guiding Matilda back towards the first greenhouse.

'Do you sell them? I've never seen anything like that.'

'No, originally we thought we could do something commercial, but actually, the fruit's too bitter. It's as though all the sweetness goes into the nectar and the flowers. So, anyway, we grow them for the glory of God. Because God gave them to us. He gives us the nectar. Don't you think that's just a beautiful idea? To grow something for God?'

Matilda didn't know what to say. Perhaps it was a beautiful idea, but the sudden fervour was disconcerting. She could feel the sweat all over her body now. A tiny bee buzzed around her head and she weakly brushed it away.

'Oh, I'm so sorry,' said Maggie, her hand resting on Matilda's arm with a tingle of static. 'I shouldn't speak like that. Of course, you may not feel like that at all. I *am* sorry – I didn't mean to crowd you. God means everything to me, but I do understand that not everyone feels like that. Forget I said anything. I'm embarrassed now.'

She didn't look embarrassed. Just cool, sweatless, her smile close to Matilda's face.

'Don't be,' said Matilda. 'Really. I suppose you're lucky feeling like that.'

'Yes, well, God helped me when I most needed it. He saved me. You see, I lost . . .' She stopped. Stood absolutely still for a moment, her face seeming shocked, frozen. And then she relaxed, softened. 'How funny! Normally I can speak about this quite easily now but somehow with you I feel . . . I don't know.' Her voice hung in the air, like a drip not quite ready to fall, needing a nudge.

'What?' Matilda heard herself asking.

Maggie picked up a scrubbing brush and handed another to Matilda. 'Let's get working while we talk, otherwise people will wonder what on earth we've been doing all morning. Anyway,' she continued, busying herself with the brush, dipping it into a bowl of soapy water, mechanically and efficiently cleaning the pots arrayed in front of her. Matilda did the same. Their eyes did not meet as Maggie continued with what she had been going to say.

Words fell like icicle spears. 'I lost my sister,' she began. And the ground beneath Matilda slipped as blackness crashed over her. In the next instant, she took control of herself again, clutching the table edge.

But Maggie had noticed. Perhaps heard the gasp. Perhaps felt the air sucked away from them. 'Hey, are you all right? Here, sit down.' She pulled out a stool and made Matilda sit down.

'I'm fine, I'm fine, I'm fine,' Matilda stumbled, the words blurring over one another until she didn't know if she was saying them or hearing their echoes in the sapping heat. Her head cleared quickly. With all these plants, she must be breathing pure oxygen. 'I'm fine,' she repeated, more clearly. 'It's just the heat and . . . and . . . what you said. How you . . . I . . .' She couldn't continue.

'Have you lost someone?' asked Maggie. Her breath was close against Matilda's ear, the warm Muscat smell of her enveloping Matilda too, drawing her in.

Words would not come. Words were not there. Instead, only emotion balled itself into a choking mass and stuck in her chest, stopping her breathing, stopping her blood, stopping her being. If she could breathe, she could cry it out. But when she opened her mouth, nothing happened.

'You have, haven't you?'

Matilda only nodded, blindly, underwater. 'You poor thing,' said Maggie. But Maggie did not understand. This was not about losing someone. Matilda had not *lost* her brother. She had never *had* her brother. He hadn't belonged to her at all. He had belonged to her parents and when he had died no one had once asked her how she felt. And, if they had, she couldn't have told them the truth because what she felt was jealousy and hatred. And Maggie would never understand that. Jealousy and hatred? Ugly words and ugly, ugly thoughts. And that was why Matilda could never speak through the ugly words that blocked her breathing. And that was why she never had said it. And that was why, whatever the psychiatrist said about how one day she would be free of it, she knew in a horrible hopeless part of her that she could never be free of it.

Maggie simply hadn't a clue. Matilda was on her own and always would be.

Maggie spoke. 'It's the jealousy, isn't it? Sometimes even hatred.'

The sun disappeared. Or maybe it already had. Maybe she just hadn't noticed before. The greenhouse lost none of its clammy heat, simply breathed sweat. The plants seemed slightly to flinch. As if they could smell the shock on Matilda's breath. The taste like fear.

How did Maggie know? How could she know? How, with so few words, could she have blasted her way into the dark secret in Matilda's heart? Matilda stood up, drew away.

The shadow was rushing towards her feet, so she turned aside. Face the light. Don't look behind.

'I don't know what you mean,' she said, looking straight into Maggie's eyes. Maggie looked back. 'I've finished these now,' continued Matilda. 'What next?'

'Well,' said Maggie, as though nothing had happened, 'I'm afraid there's more over here. Oh, there's the rain again.' The rain began to batter on the greenhouse roof like stones, a drumbeat as loud as their voices. It was surreal, the way the weather changed up here. As though the laws of nature span with another will.

Being silent was easier with this noise clattering around them. Matilda began to breathe once more. She almost wanted to talk again, wanting Maggie to take her back to the edge, wanted to be pushed over so that someone could catch her and take responsibility. She felt as if she had walked on to the edge of a cliff, the wind had gusted and she had so nearly lost her footing. But just how bad would it have been to fall?

'I'm sorry,' said Maggie, after a few moments. 'If you don't want to talk, that's fine. But just so you know, we're here if you want us. We can help, you know. Help you find a way through. It might not be the same for you as it is for me. But I know I was saved. And now I can talk about it and breathe and live. And we can do that for you.'

Matilda didn't know what to say. All the things she might have said churned and blended into each other at the edges of her mind but she couldn't disentangle the ones that would work.

'Thanks. I'll . . . think. But thanks.' And she meant it. The warmth that came from Maggie was something that was hard to say no to.

They worked on. Maggie asked her about her school, exams, her waiting university place, showed interest in her plan to go to South America. Matilda asked Maggie about her own childhood.

'I don't think about it. It's behind me. It wasn't happy. I was not the person I am now. I have a new family now. This is my home. This is where all the people who love me are. You have to stay with people who love you, love you for what you are, not for what they wish you were. People who don't judge. People who help you grow. Everything I need is here. God is here.'

When she said that, when she made this extraordinarily huge and yet simple statement, this absurdly empty yet vitally full point, something reached into Matilda's heart and touched her, like a tentacle of distant knowledge. Like something watching her, even waiting for her. It was as though she had heard it before and yet never listened to it before.

'Let's stop for a cup of tea,' said Maggie after a while. 'You stay here, just finish up these last trays, and I'll go and get us some tea. If the sun comes out we can sit outside. Be back soon.'

And she was gone. Suddenly everything was back to normal. Matilda shook her head in confusion. All this God-talk. How weird was that? What was she doing even thinking about God? She'd had God rammed down her throat since she could remember. Mind you, her parents' God didn't seem like this girl's God. Her parents' God only worked on Sundays, or funeral days and weddings. This God seemed to work overtime. This God was, apparently, everywhere. Her parents' God stayed safe inside His church worrying about silly details.

The rain had stopped again, she noticed. The steam rose in the greenhouses and Matilda brushed the damp hair from her face. She heard a crunch on the gravel outside, turned to see Maggie, with a tray, talking to someone. Matilda couldn't see who it was but the person walked away. Then the door opened and Maggie came in.

'Let's go out, shall we, Matilda? It's sunny again and I've got a couple of towels to dry some seats.'

Matilda followed her out, shielding her eyes against the full sunlight, and was glad to be away from that laden air. A light breeze cooled the sweat on her face. She followed Maggie over to some wooden seats and helped her dry them off before they both sat down.

The tea did not taste like normal tea. 'Passionflower and peach,' said Maggie, in answer to Matilda's expression. 'Hope you like it. Cake?' Matilda expected carrot cake or something dryly healthy, but no – this was a rich, moist, shining, gooey chocolate cake, thick with butter-cream filling and fudge icing. And the tea, surprisingly, was delicious, refreshing and just sweet enough. She drank it thirstily.

Almost immediately, she felt a wave of relaxation. It started from her toes and flooded up through her stomach, heart, head. She closed her eyes, turning her face towards the mid-morning sun, smelling the recent rain on the grass. Maggie started talking and Matilda nodded drowsily. Maggie seemed to be talking about the fruit farm laid out below them down the hillside and along the valley. Matilda tried to concentrate, tried to nod at the right times, occasionally to say something sensible. She heard the crunch of gravel as someone came towards them and she knew she would have to open her eyes and be introduced.

She did, stood up, smiled, held out her hand, shook the hand that was offered, answered something in answer to the question that was asked, smiled again, sat down, closed her eyes again. But couldn't remember for the life of her whom she had seen, what she had said, what the person had said. Was aware only of a smile, from him, or her, from the world: she didn't know or mind or need to know.

Everything floated on a smile and the smell of strawberries swelled more thickly than she had ever known. And long, cinnamon dreams of sand and sea and water between toes and drifty hair and watery bubbles around her head. Ripples in her mind, feathers on her skin, sweet candyfloss breath, ice on her tongue tip. And words – those were the bubbles – words blowing from her mouth and dancing gently in the breeze, blown-glass rainbows in the light, and disappearing. She smiled. Drifted further. Away.

Into a dream. But in her dream she could feel every part of her, as though she were awake. She knew she was on the terrace outside the big house, sitting in the sun. That she was drinking passionflower and peach tea and eating chocolate cake with a girl who talked about God. Yet she was dreaming too, the theta rhythms merging with reality.

In her dream she was outside that house again, the ancient walls oozing cold and damp, and the seeping smell of decay. But the smell washed away as she approached, and was replaced by something bright and red. Passionflower-red, licking its way up the walls like flames. In the way of dreams, she realised without surprise that this was now not the same house as before. This was the house on the hill. She walked up to it. This was Heaven and she was looking in. Here was the window and through it the scene: the man and the woman beside the bed, dressed in their best clothes, beautiful and shining and privileged. Weeping by the bed of their son. Matilda knew she had to look at the bed and in a daze she did. And was strangely unsurprised to see no boy in the bed. Her brother was not there.

In her half-dream, she turned and ran, flying down the hill through the warm rain. And she knew in a part of her that she mustn't turn round, at the same time as knowing that she would. Because you always do. Because you have to and yet you must not. And when she did, she saw him there, at the top of the hill, by the house. Calling her. Her brother, with long golden Jesus hair and a white robe and sandals.

'Come with me, Matilda. It is time. It is time to go. Come on, Matilda.' And she ran towards him now, running up the hill again towards what she saw there. In her dream now, she did run towards her brother.

'Matilda, it is time to go. Come on, Matilda.' She was only halfway to the top of the hill but she was being woken, gently, by Maggie, touching her arm softly and letting her hand linger there as she rocked her awake. Kindly smiling.

The feeling of being wrapped up. It almost suffocated her.

She was left with an intense sensation of calm. As if there was nothing to worry about. As if one day she would get to the top of the hill in her dream. And that when she did, everything would be all right.

'You fell asleep!' said Maggie. 'It must be the sun. Either that or I am much more boring than I thought!'

'Sorry! I'm really sorry,' said Matilda. 'I guess I'm tired. How embarrassing!'

'Don't be silly. You looked very peaceful. And it was only a few minutes. But I think we need to get going. You need to get back down to the hostel – it'll be the normal rota now. The sun's set to stay. Not a cloud to be seen.'

And she was right. There wasn't.

# 12

# F is for Falling

Later that afternoon, Matilda picked strawberries and made sensible conversation with people as they all crouched or stooped or squatted uncomfortably along the rows. There was no comfortable way to pick strawberries, she realised now.

George was in her group and every now and then she passed close enough to him that she had to speak. She didn't look at him properly. Why did she feel awkward? She hadn't done anything wrong, but she felt his disapproval. What did that matter? Who was he, anyway? Just another fruit-picker. She avoided his eyes and simply made comments about the heat or the pains in her knees or how she could happily never see another strawberry as long as she lived. He made similar conversation back.

But when their shift ended, and she took a cup of tea from the hostel and went to drink it outside to avoid talking to anyone at all, she found herself with George again. He had been standing by a tree, drinking his tea, and she hadn't seen him till it was too late.

'Hi, Matilda,' he said.

'Hi, George.' Both of them looked awkwardly away from each other.

'So, what's it like up there?' he asked, coming straight to the point after a few moments.

'The house?' Yes, of course the house. He didn't even bother to nod, just took another mouthful of his tea and wiped his lips with the back of his hand. 'I wasn't in the house,' she said.

'Oh?'

'I just had to clean some stuff in the greenhouses, that's all. Maggie took me there, Maggie cleaned the stuff with me, and then we came back.'

'Why?'

'Why what? Why did I clean stuff? Because Maggie asked me to and she's the boss. What are you getting at?'

'Did you do anything else while you were up there?'

'Like what? Hey, what are all the questions for, George? I haven't done anything. I've just done what I was told.'

'Keep your voice down,' he said, quietly, without looking at her. 'Did you eat or drink anything when you were up there?'

She looked at him now. 'What do you mean?'

'Which bit don't you understand? Did you eat or drink anything up there?'

'Sod you – I don't like the way you say that. What do you mean, "which bit don't you understand?" That's bloody patronising. What's it to you whether I had anything to eat or drink up there?'

'Did you? Tell me, Matilda.'

She was about to snap at him again but something in the way he looked at her, something in his eyes, made her answer. 'Yes, I had some fruit tea and some chocolate cake.'

'Shit.'

'What do you mean? George! What's wrong?'

'Matilda, please don't go there again.'

'Oh, for crying out loud! What's the sodding mystery, George? You're really bugging me! You and Matt, you're both the same. Yes, OK, they're maybe what you'd call religious nutters, but they didn't try to pressurise me and – for Christ's sake! – I drank fruit tea and ate chocolate cake and look! Look at my arms – oh my God, green spots!'

Her eyes blazed as she laughed at him. 'They were nice to me, George. They didn't judge or criticise or any of the crap that I'm used to.'

'They sent Matt away, didn't they? Was that about not judging? I heard they busted him for drugs. I heard you were getting close to him. I heard he was prying into what they were doing. And the next day he has to leave. Hmm, just coincidences, eh?'

'It wasn't their fault! Matt knew what the rules were!' Why was she defending them? Against Matt? What was that about? But she was angry. Maggie had made her feel wanted, relaxed. And it was obvious there was nothing going on up at the house on the hill. Just some people who were happy together and who ran a fruit farm as a business. So what if they were religious? So what if that's what they chose to believe? They hadn't tried to convert her, had they? There had been no pressure at all.

What right did boring George have to come along with his suspicions and his patronising questions?

They stood in tension, their tea going cold. The sun now was veiled in drifts of gauzy cloud, the late afternoon settling into torpor and the day's sweat chilling on their skin.

'Anyway,' she said. 'What was that about eating and drinking anything? You think they drugged me?' And as she said it, a sudden fear pinpricked her skin – had she been drugged? She had fallen into that weird dream-state immediately after drinking the tea, hadn't she? She had felt so relaxed – could there have been something in the tea? That was ridiculous! It was just a fruit tea and it was well known that herbal or fruit teas could be very relaxing, good for stress. And she had been stressed, tired, depressed, hot. It was hardly surprising, after all the turmoil of the last few days, if she fell asleep in the sun after drinking some fruit tea, was it?

Besides, it had made her feel good. What was wrong with that? It was only tea.

'You want to know?'

'Don't be so bloody irritating, George. You're obviously dying to tell me.'

'There was a girl called Jemima. Last year. Here. She used to go up to the house sometimes. She told me they used to give her fruit tea and chocolate cake. She went weird and, after a while, she disappeared.'

'Disappeared? You mean she left?'

'No, she didn't leave. She's up there in the house now.'

'How do you know?'

'Can you keep a secret?'

'Piss off and don't be patronising. Of course I can keep a secret if it's important.'

'I went there. Two weeks ago. At night. I looked through the window. I saw them. They were in a circle. There was a bowl of fire, bit weird, just in a bowl, with no sticks or coals or anything, and sort of bluey flames. And Jemima was there, dressed like them. And they were having some sort of ceremony, all kneeling down with their hands outstretched and their eyes shut.'

Matilda could see one of the Lilies walking towards them behind George.

'I think you'll find it's called praying, George. You should be more tolerant.'

The Lily was close now. It was one Matilda had never seen. Thick beautiful hair like the rest of them. A soft air of calm and strength. A way of walking that used the least possible energy. Wasting nothing.

George shrugged his shoulders. Hardened his face. He had not seen the Lily approaching. Matilda gave no sign that she had either. 'OK, Matilda. I get the message. Enjoy your new friends. I'm sorry Matt left, I'm sorry your other friends left, and I'm sorry about whatever it is that makes you so defensive, but I'm just saying, be careful. Don't let them make you do something you don't want. People like that, they manipulate you. They—'

'Hello, George. And hello, Matilda, isn't it?' The Lily held out her hand and Matilda took it, feeling its warmth and cotton cleanness. 'I'm Angel.' She laughed, more with her face than with a noise, more like a flutter than a proper laugh. 'Yes, I know, I'm no angel really, but it kind of stuck – my real name's Angela.'

'Hi,' said Matilda back. 'Pleased to meet you.'

'Anyway, don't let me interrupt you,' said Angel, smiling at George. 'It looked as though you were deep in conversation. Please carry on. Don't mind me. I'll just take your mugs in, shall I?' And she took the mugs and walked slowly off.

Matilda knew perfectly well that Angel must have heard what George was saying. She also knew perfectly well that she had not tried to stop him.

She felt another sharp shiver of fear. Had she gone too far? Would George lose his job now because of her?

'Sorry,' she said quietly. 'I didn't see her coming,' she lied. And swallowed the bitter taste of guilt.


George was still there the next day. And the next. And the next. Matilda relaxed again: there was nothing to worry about.

So when Angel asked her to come up to the house on the hill, she went willingly and without fear. She looked forward to the feeling of warmth that came from Heaven. She longed to inhale the tomato heat of the hothouses and to sweat in the tropical steam amongst the enormous fruits of God's earth.

And when she drank the passionflower and peach tea and dozed and swam through the beautiful strangeness of her waking dream again, and when her brother called her – her brother with the Jesus hair and the white robe and no shadows anywhere around him – she ran, laughing again, through the warm rain towards him.

She didn't reach him before she was wakened, but she knew inside herself that one day she would.

*Part Three*

**The Year 2029**

# Prison – Two Weeks
## Before Release

The little old woman gripped the smooth squishtic steering-wheel of her bruised red Branson Mirage. She narrowed her eyes and steeled herself. The closer she came to the heart of the matter, to the end of the story, the steelier she must be. She must remember her promise to God.

She could be strong, she could, this little old woman with her well-shaped fingernails. She could listen with relish to whatever version of truth he came up with, the man with the Jesus hair. And she would not let him control her. She would save his soul. And, in this way, find a path to her own heaven.

To this she would dedicate her remaining life. With burning passion. Vengeance is mine, sayeth the Lord. Not for herself, vengeance, of course. For the Lord. Her job was simply to offer his confession and atonement to God. She must remember that, keep it high in her mind, floating above everything else, hiding all other thoughts.

She looked up at the sheet-smooth walls. She did not know which was his window. Did he watch her now? Did his eyes light with pleasure at her visit? She was probably the only one who visited him, she thought, the little old woman with her sad gecko eyes, the crinkled lids, the desert skin corrugating her cheekbones. She played with the loose rings on her fingers. She was losing weight. As though the souls she saved here were sucking the blood from her, feeding off her strength. She did not mind. This was what made her life worth living. And she was strong enough.

But after one more visit next week, she would not come back here again. The week after that he would be released. That was what she had been working towards. After that, her work would soon be done. If she could do it. If she could stay strong enough and not be swayed by his twisting words. She must not doubt that.

A few moments later she was entering the prison, passing her fingers over the security scanner that would let her in, and looking at the iris-recognition system until the green light flashed. A disembodied lilting voice spoke: 'Good afternoon, Mrs Bailey. Come through, please.' And the door slid away into nothing. And, after a few nice words with the pleasant young man in the Control Centre, and a smiling wave from several of the pale-suited Rehab officers, and a friendly stroke of the

Facilitator's cat, she was on her way, following the young female Rehab officer – young enough to be her granddaughter – along the familiar aromatic corridors.

Not that she had a granddaughter. Obviously.

As the door was opened for her, her heart twisted and her breath cracked in her chest again. He really did look like the pictures of Jesus. A light sweat broke out under her arms. She smiled at him.

'Good afternoon, Peter. How are you today?'

He held out his hands towards her, though both of them remembered they could not touch. His eyes glistened slightly, softened, and he smiled back at her. It was enough to make a woman melt.

A Rehab officer brought them some tea. He was young and soft-faced, dressed in pale blue and with pink-tipped hair and one of those tiny, coloured facial tattoos that were the fashion, just above one eyebrow. Better than those piercings that used to be all the rage, she thought.

'Here you are, Mrs B,' he said. 'Will you be Mother?'

'Aren't I always?' she replied, smiling sweetly, as though the reference to motherhood had passed her by. The truth of that particular situation was one she preferred to keep hidden. It was not for these men to know.

She poured the tea with a steady hand. Peter watched

the rings glinting, one heavy diamond on her wedding finger, three on another ring on her right hand. There must be several thousand pounds' worth of diamonds there, he thought, as often before. What could you do with several thousand pounds? You could do God's work with that.

'Well, Peter. Only two weeks to go now. How are you feeling?' She looked at him and smiled.

He could see the soft hairs on her old face. That was what his mother's skin had been like when she died. Though his mother had died poor, not encrusted with jewels and coiffed by pampering and swathed in expensive tailored clothes.

'A little nervous, Sarah. More than a little nervous. They've taken me out a few times, you know, to get used to things. The world is so different now. I hardly recognised anything, even from the television. Everything is so fast. People even speak fast. And it seems you can go through your day without talking to people, just machines. They showed me how you buy something without any money or card or anything, in one of those eye things – whatever you call it – and I did it without speaking to a human. It was unnatural.'

'It's still God's world, Peter. That hasn't changed, you know.'

132

His face lit up. 'Trust you to say just the right thing, Sarah. Yes, of course, it is still God's world.'

'And He still smiles in it.'

His face sank. A cloud passed behind his eyes. 'But will He smile on me, Sarah? You know, sometimes I am so full of doubt. You see, I *thought* I was doing the right thing before. I thought God was telling me what to do. But I now understand that I was misled, by the Devil. The Devil made me do those things. Why else the fire? Why else the death? But what will happen when God seems to speak to me again? How will I know if it is really God?'

'Because you are better now. And you have paid the price for what you did,' she said, mechanically.

'Is it enough, though, Sarah? All those deaths. All that fire. What if God hasn't punished me enough?'

She looked at his face. Was this the truth? This remorse. Was it real? His feather-soft fingers were loose around his plastic cup. Motionless. His face looked down, his eyes half hidden from her by his blond lashes. His pale hair with its ashen edges was like a veil, hanging around his shoulders. She was surprised that he had been allowed to grow it. That would never have been allowed in the old days.

The bright light from above cast no shadows in the room. Everywhere was light.

'God is good, Peter. God will judge and God will decide. But you must look inside yourself and know yourself and believe that you have washed away all the badness. You must. Then you will know that God has forgiven you. And remember, Jesus died for you.' The familiar words sounded comforting and flowed easily from her lips.

Now he looked up again, meeting her eyes. Those delicate, pale-blue eyes. For a moment he just looked at her – a long moment. It was as though she had said something wrong, and he was deciding whether to put her right.

'You are good to me, Sarah. You are a good woman. You have been such a help to me. I wish you could help me after I leave this place.' His smooth, milky voice played over her ears and face like cotton-wool fingers. She felt it drawing her breath from her. How did he manage to control her breathing?

She must be tough, she must.

She must not let him weave her thoughts with his flat tapeworm fingers and his spindle words. They had warned her about this. And certainly, the way he looked at you was enough to melt the stoniest heart. As hers was. She felt herself begin to melt. Felt the air between them sweeten and become heavy like a blanket ready to wrap her up. Everyone wants to be wrapped up. It is always tempting to let go. Even to let go of what you really believe in.

Maybe he really had atoned. Maybe she could trust him now. And trust God to judge. Maybe her role in all this really was over and she should let go, satisfied that he had paid the price and that God would do the rest.

It used to be so easy to put God before everything else, and to trust Him. And when he had sometimes let her down in the distant past, she had told herself it was only to test her. That was what people always did say to explain why, if God is good, He brings so much pain to innocent people. But it was hard to believe sometimes – quite impossible sometimes – and how she had struggled with that! But, having made her choice, she must hold herself strong now, not let the doubts creep in to sway her purpose.

'Perhaps I can. Perhaps I can help.'

He looked at her face. He could smell her old woman scent, slightly too sweet, like a peach that is over-ripe and ready to collapse in on itself. The skin was shrivelled but soft, too. He looked at her jewellery. How could she live with herself, he thought, with her talk of God and forgiveness and heaven and still wear God's jewels around her skinny fingers? His mother would not have done that.

'Perhaps I can,' she said again.

'Bless you, Sarah. But no, you can't. I must do this myself.' He rubbed his forehead hard with the tips of his fingers, as though he had a headache.

'What is it you want to do?'

'I want . . . sorry, I must forget the idea. It's impossible. I would never be allowed.'

'What is it?'

'No.' But it was not a strong 'no'. It left room for doubt.

'Peter, you must say. Perhaps I *can* help. Anything is possible.' She wanted to know what his idea was, whatever it might be. She wanted to know everything in his heart. She watched his fingers as they pressed into his temples. He brushed his hair back from his face. Just below the hairline, she could see some pale marks. Scars. Why had she never noticed those before?

'It's for children, Sarah. That's why I want to do it. I want to help children. Do you understand?'

No, she did not understand. She certainly did not. She narrowed her eyes, held tight to her feelings, and looked straight back at him. 'You'll need to explain, Peter.'

'I want to help children. I thought, well, I thought if I rebuild the house, it could be a place for children. For their holidays. For disadvantaged children. You know?' He looked at her from beneath his eyelashes, hesitantly, as if afraid she might laugh at him. She would have, if she hadn't been so trapped by his eyes and the thoughts in her head.

He went on, speaking more quickly now. You might almost think he had planned this, had rehearsed everything he would say. 'Of course, no one must know it was me. That would be important. I would have to be discreet.' He looked over to the Rehab officer, behind the glass, but with the sliding window slightly open. The man was gouging stuff from under his fingernails with a blue nailfile and watching a portable movie-player. Peter lowered his voice further, just in case. 'It would have to be someone else at the head of the project.'

She said nothing. She knew what he was saying, the little old woman with her not-so-stupid eyes. And she would not do it. Never. She would save his soul in another way but not that.

Would she?

Into the silence came his smooth vanilla voice again, oozing its way into her head. You could almost imagine him saying, 'Blessed are those who truly repent and turn to Him. Blessed are those who travail and are heavy-laden, for I will make them whole.'

'You see, Sarah,' he said, and his hands stretched towards hers, though they did not touch. They stayed a few small centimetres away, resting light as wafers on the curved lilac table. 'You see, I need to do something. It is not enough to assume forgiveness, to take it as my right. I must do something. And I must confess—' he paused '—that it is for myself, too. It is for my own childhood. You see, I suffered so much. Oh, I don't want to go on about it and I do want to move forward. But my childhood was so difficult and I know there are other children out there who suffer too. If I could only help them, I believe it would help them and help me too. To come to terms with everything myself.'

He rubbed his finger over his forehead again and again she saw those pale scars.

'Do you want to tell me about it, Peter? Your childhood?' she asked. 'Perhaps it might help to talk.' He must spill his heart to her and through her to God. He must go over the rosary of his suffering. She had promised God that He would judge but she too wanted to watch Peter remember it, to watch him suffer it again. Because he deserved that, he did. He must atone – before her and before God.

What if she were swayed to pity him? To forgive him? She smiled inwardly at the absurd thought. It was not for her to pity nor forgive. If she were God, she would do neither, but she was not God.

She relished the test of her will. She would never let him manipulate her. It would be the other way round. Not so innocent, the eyes of that little old woman. No, not so innocent. Not so weak. She turned her eyes from him and looked at her hands. She played with the rings. How sad her hands looked, she thought. How dry and dusty and thin and sad. She looked at her rings. The safety of wealth. But no amount of money could buy you happiness. You had to do other things for that. You had to search for it and it had to be hard to find. For her it was, very hard. But she knew how she would find it. Through Peter. Peter with his Jesus hair and his wafer fingers and his heaven eyes and his lips the colour of crushed raspberries.

He began to speak. And as he spoke, eloquently, softly, sadly, she felt she could picture the scene exactly.

*The son, a thin seven years old, stood with his bare feet in the mud outside the kitchen door. The snow that had fallen in the night had turned to sludge. His stomach still hurt, the muscles wrenched from the vomiting. But it was his fault. He should never have stolen the chocolate cake, should never have gorged himself, should never have lost control so entirely. The fact that it was his mother's birthday cake only made it worse. She did not deserve such a bad boy.*

*She was good. His mother was good. He should never have*

*eaten her birthday cake. Honour thy father and mother. Thou shalt not steal their chocolate cakes.*

*It was right that he should be standing out here in the slush, in the dark, in the sleeting rain. It was right that he should stand here till his feet froze.*

*The boy turned towards the house, looked at the warm apricot light that blushed from the window where his parents stood. A slight nod from his father. His mother clasped her hands together. And the boy walked to where he knew he must. To the bottom of the garden. To where the ancient apple trees stood as shadows in the orchard, their empty branches like arthritic fingers clawing at the wind.*

*He felt nothing now in his feet. He should feel something. He should feel the cold. He should feel the pain.*

*Under the apple trees he must kneel in the sodden grass, feeling the wet against his bare legs. And he must close his eyes and pray. Which he did. He forced himself to pray, and not to think about the wet and cold and his parents watching him from the house. He rocked and prayed, just as he had been taught. If he prayed hard enough he would be forgiven.*

*He could almost pray hard enough − almost − if he tried painfully hard to ignore the terrible need to listen for the sound of the mother and father coming for him. But not quite, not quite could he block out the thoughts and concentrate on the praying. If he tried harder, if only he could try harder, be a better boy . . .*

*Soon, he heard the door of the house bang shut. He did not hear his parents walk towards him across the garden but he knew they were coming. A tear squeezed its way down a cheek. He carried on praying, trying. No more denying.*

*Now the mother and father were there and the son held out his hands as he knew he must. He felt the sharp pain as the object was placed gently on his head and pressed down hard, harder. He felt blood drip down his face from where the thorns had pierced his forehead. Knew it was blood because it was warm, not cold like the sleety rain. And the blood and the tears and the ice mixed into pale juice and flowed down his face and tasted sweet when he licked his lips.*

*Then the mother and the father knelt and prayed with their son. For their son. Ice-like pain shot through their knees, but still they prayed. Their muscles became rigid, but they did not stop praying. Their fingers and bare feet became cold and then numb, but still they never stopped loving their only son and praying.*

The little old woman sat in her dented red sports car. With her hands on the worn squishtic steering-wheel, she leaned back in the seat and breathed out, long and hard.

She picked up the small bunch of sweet peas which the prison officer had given her. From Peter's garden. Buried her face in their soft petals, inhaled the freshness.

You could get drunk on such a scent. She closed her eyes.

It was a terrible story.

She smiled.

It was a terrible and beautiful story. But was it enough? She wanted more. She wanted to drink in the story of his suffering and watch him relive it all, feeling the pain of it again. And she wanted to test herself, and God, to the limit. Then they would see who was strongest.

A grin spread over Peter's face. He had done it! He was sure the stupid old bat had fallen for it. He could probably do with an extra week to be on the safe side, but he was sure that next week, he'd be able to persuade her to part with her address at least. Or some other information that would allow him to find where she lived. Then he would be able to get her full trust. And with no one else to leave her money to, he would be able to persuade her to help him. He knew it.

And it would all begin again. He could smell the raspberries now, the scorched bitter smell of them burning. Could taste the tempranillo heat of the plastic tunnels before they dripped into molten pools on the ground. Could see the lines of strawberries, the flames racing through the straw, spiralling towards the house.

He could hear the tomato-shrieks of breaking glass in the greenhouses, remembered the peculiar screams of melons as they burst. He saw it now: a sea of glass, mingled with fountains of fire.

The fruits of his labours. Of His labours. Because it was what God wanted. His Father.

Peter was His son. He knew what God wanted. He did not need some cracked old woman with gecko eyes to tell him who had forgiven whom.

Honour thy father and mother.

Peter knelt by his bed. And the words were silent in his head, but he heard them. 'Blessed are the dead which die in the Lord from henceforth: Yea, sayeth the Spirit, that they may rest from their labours and their works do follow them.'

God spoke to Peter and His word was good.

Peter smiled as he prayed and felt the fruits of his labours begin to spring slowly from their seeds. He tasted them on his skin, smelled them sweeten his breath.

Now when he prayed, he prayed well and no disturbing thoughts could worm their way in. Now Peter was good.

Now his mother and his father would be proud of him.

*Part Four*

**The Year 2004**

# 1

# T is for Temptation

It wasn't raining the next time Matilda went to Heaven. It was David who took her there. He came to her as she was leaving the hostel with the others, ready to go up to the fields. She felt the awkward silence from them as he called over to her.

'Matilda! Would you mind coming up to the house today? We need you there again.' The 'again' settled into the air, wasp-like and unpleasant, and she wished the others hadn't had to hear. And that she hadn't sensed George's tightening shoulders.

Why should she mind? What did George matter? Only that he was an anchor to the sensible side of her, the side that knew that the people up in the house were not really like her. She was torn between two paths, and George was the one who pulled her his way. Her way? The sensible way? The right way?

The boring way. The way that would lead her back to everything she knew so well. And wanted to escape from. Into anything. And David and Angel and Maggie and Rachel, whoever they all were, however unlike her they were, offered something strange and exciting. But they offered more than that, much more than that, though it was only when she was up there, in the house on the hill, that she remembered what it was. The beautiful waking dream that drew her further in each time. And now, standing there in the early morning chill, she had nearly forgotten the feeling, and almost wanted to stay with George and the others and be normal. Comfortably, sadly normal.

But gorgeous David was calling her, and everyone knew you did what the Beautiful People told you. Even if no one but George could explain why. So she shrugged and slightly smiled at the others and called 'Sure' to David, picking up her bag and walking towards him.

The sun shone strongly as they bumped up the path in David's still-battered car. He smelled of soap and bread and warm muscle and clean man.

He turned to her, smiled in that heart-tingling way. 'So, Matilda, how are you doing? You're looking well. The suntan suits you.' And his eyes lingered on her face just fractionally, deliciously long.

'Yeah, good, thanks. Settling in.'

'Making friends? I know your other friends left. You OK about that?'

Matilda hesitated. David noticed because he looked over at her again. A large pothole interrupted what she might have said and they both winced as their bodies rattled.

'No,' David continued, 'I guess you're not OK. Don't worry – always takes a while to make new friends. And we'll look after you. Maggie says we could use you more in the greenhouses, that you have a natural way with plants. Green-fingers, eh? You've done that sort of stuff before? She said something about tomatoes.'

What had Maggie said about tomatoes?

'Yeah, well I can't say I had much success with tomatoes, actually. My mother has a greenhouse though. She spends a lot of time in it and she grows tomatoes; so I suppose I picked stuff up from her.'

There was a silence. Words flashed through Matilda's mind, but none of them seemed adequate or right. Or small enough for such a little space. David was the one who spoke.

'So, tell me about your parents. What do they do?'

'Good,' said Matilda. It just came out like that, surprising herself with its vehemence.

'Sorry?'

'Good. They do good. It's what they're good at.'

'Hey, I'm struggling here,' said David, turning to her

with a smile. 'They do good? But you don't sound happy about it. Er, good is good, isn't it?'

Christ, why was she getting into this? Here she was in a car for five minutes with the most dumbstrikingly gorgeous guy and she was starting to tell him about her parents, frankly the last topic she wanted to get into on a sunny day with heaven before her.

'Yeah, sorry, ignore me. I was just being flip. It's just that my parents do make rather a *thing* out of being good.' She held her breath, as though by saying the next bit without breathing she could say it without breaking, and the words rushed out without her trying or being able to stop them. 'They lost a child, years ago, and they never got over it. They think the more good they do the better they'll feel. I don't think it works. They don't know how to be happy.'

And you do? David never said it but the question hung in the air. And now the car was scrunching up to the back of the house and she was undoing her seatbelt, glad to get away. If she'd stayed sitting there a moment longer, he'd have asked her, she knew he would. David unfolded himself from the car and went quickly round to hold the door for her. She climbed out, almost blushing. Not looking at him.

She knew that what she had said was enormous. She wished she hadn't said it. She had given David a piece of information which he must follow up. Or else store inside him and know her weakness.

He flustered her. His unreachable perfection made her feel entirely inadequate and small. Could he not have some blemish that perhaps she hadn't noticed, something unattractive? Then it would be easier to talk to him. Maybe some spots to spoil him? She looked at his face out of the corner of her eye as they walked towards the greenhouses. No spots. She felt herself begin to sweat. What was she getting into? Why had she dropped hints about her parents and then, for God's sake, blurted out the bit about them losing a child? And she might as well have painted an enormous arrow pointing towards her own loss.

Maybe she hadn't said it? Maybe she had imagined it and it was just a voice in her head? After all, it wasn't something she made of a habit of telling people. It's not the sort of thing you want to go into. She'd done it with Maggie, but that was different. Not exactly good, either, but Maggie was a woman and women didn't so much mind hearing heart stuff, did they?

She heard herself making comments about the pots of spherical bay trees and pink geraniums and ornamental roses and herbs and every bloody beautiful growing thing she could see. Anything to blot out the cliff-edge conversation she had accidentally begun.

The gluey air wrapped itself around her head and she could hear the warm blood-beat in her ears. Above her danced the bluest sky and around her fell the heat. Her thoughts hung.

They walked in odd silence towards the greenhouses. At least, the silence felt odd to Matilda and she could only assume he felt the same. But for all she knew, David might have been thinking about something entirely different. The void between them was crossable only by a thin, wobbling bridge.

He opened the door before her, and this time she was ready for the heat as it hit her. Beautiful, gasping, deliciously nearly unbearable. And within a few seconds she was wrapped up in it. She wished she could never leave.

'So, what are we doing today?'

'Feeding. Everything. Weekly feed. None of these chemical slow-release things that modern farms use. We make this ourselves with organic compounds and sugar and a secret ingredient.'

She looked questioningly at him.

'Prayer.' He said it simply, looking at her with that skin-crackling tiny smile, and she swiftly turned away, embarrassed and determined not to show it.

'Oh, right, yeah, figures. And it obviously works,' she said, trying to keep any flippancy out of her voice as she looked around the massive greenhouse with its tomatoes ripening on plants bigger than any she'd ever seen. And actually, flippant though she might have felt, she couldn't help wondering if perhaps they were right.

Up here, in here, with these people, you could bring yourself to believe in miracles.

David showed her how to mix the various ingredients, all from dark brown bottles. He worked calmly, easily, fluidly. Counting spoonsful of this and spoonsful of that, drops of something and drips of something else. *Oh my God*, she thought, suddenly. *What about the praying bit? He's not going to do the praying bit now, is he? No, please say he's not going to do it.*

At home, they'd once had a minister with a disconcerting habit of wanting to pray out loud every time he came to their house. Which was often, after her brother had died. She remembered once she had been hiding and peeking out from behind the sofa and her father had offered the minister a whisky and the minister had taken it and then shut his eyes and prayed aloud, with his hands outstretched, the whisky still in one hand. And his eyes were crinkled shut so tightly, as though he could only see God when his eyes were tight shut, not out in the real world where there were such random distractions as whisky and death rituals and grieving parents.

And when the minister had opened his eyes he had looked straight at her, as though, when he was talking to God inside his head, God had told him she was there. And her father had been cross that she was there and had asked her to go and find her mother. But her mother was crying in the kitchen and you could tell from the wailing nature of her sobbing that she did not want Matilda to come in and see her then. Or maybe she did but Matilda didn't want to see her mother crying. Because you don't, do you? Your mother crying is absolutely the last thing you want to see when you are a small child. What you need is someone to notice you crying yourself.

Now here was someone else who was going to pray out loud in front of her. And this time she might have to join in. She started to blush already and feel the embarrassment prickle her skin.

When he had finished pouring and measuring, he picked up the container with the home-made fertiliser and looked at her. 'Well? You ready?'

'What?'

'To get these tomatoes fed. One scoop per two litres of water, two litres of water per plant, at the roots and the surrounding soil to about twenty centimetres.'

'Oh right, sorry.' But you couldn't keep anything to yourself with these people. They could read your mind.

'You thought I was going to say a prayer, didn't you?' The amusement in his voice made her feel small again.

'Well, you said . . .'

'Yeah, but I was praying while I was doing it. Don't always have to make a special issue of it. My work is my prayer to God.'

Cringe. Cringe. *Cringe*. Why did they have to speak like that?

And yet . . .

'Sorry, I've gone a bit over the top, haven't I? No, seriously, I'm really sorry. I shouldn't assume you feel like me. I know this God talk can sound weird. It did to me once.' They began to measure fertiliser into watering cans and, in turn, to fill them from the tap.

'What did you do before you came here?' she asked, to make conversation and fill the space, and because talking to him was becoming easier than she had expected.

'Bad. I did bad. Bad stuff. You said your parents do good. I did bad.'

'Like?'

'Drugs. I didn't care about anything. I didn't use what God gave me. I drifted, I took. I gave nothing to anyone. Except abuse when they didn't do what I wanted.'

'So what happened?'

'A friend died. Overdose. Accidental. But I had supplied the heroin. I was there when she died. I didn't notice. I was high myself at the time.' David stopped, watering can in hand, and Matilda looked at him, not knowing what to say. He continued. 'Did some time in prison, got a place in rehab, got myself clean. Then one of the volunteers in the rehab place told me about Peter.'

'Peter?'

'Our leader.' The man with the long white robe. The one who sent shadows rushing from his fingers, David said, 'He saved me. Simply. And now I do good, not bad.' He smiled at her, properly now, but now he no longer looked perfect and golden and impossible. He was blemished after all. And human.

David continued, filling his watering can again. 'And I'd die for him. We all would.' His words held a fervour that Matilda could tell was real. She wished she could feel like that, that passionate, that real, that trusting.

'I'd even . . .' But she never heard what he was going to say, because just then the door opened and in came Maggie and Angel.

They beamed as they walked towards David and Matilda. 'Hey, you two! How're you doing?' and they both came quickly up to Matilda and hugged her.

Hugged David. All of them looked at Matilda, their attention making her feel different. Which, of course, she was.

'No, really, Matilda, how *are* you?' said Maggie. 'Now that your friends have gone? Are you OK? Really OK?' When they asked questions, these people, they really did seem to want the answers. It was not some polite formula.

'Yeah, fine, I'm fine. Thanks.'

'Well you know, anything you want, any time you're feeling low, you know – just come and see us. You're always welcome.' Maggie held Matilda's eyes in the warmth of her own.

'Oh, David,' Angel said suddenly, 'Peter wanted to know if you've taken those cuttings. You know, the ones we talked about last night?'

David looked perplexed. Angel and Maggie both looked at him. The silence lengthened. 'You know, the tea-roses? For propagation?'

'Oh, right, yeah, sorry. Completely forgot. Matilda, can you carry on feeding the rest of the plants in the same way? And in the next two greenhouses, if you have time. Oh, I'd better open the doors for you.' He took his swipecard from his pocket and carried on talking as he walked over to the door into the next greenhouse. 'But don't let yourself get too hot in here –

the temperature in the furthest greenhouse especially can get too much after a while. Make sure you come out for some fresh air when you need it. And have you got drinking water?'

She had. And once David had come back from opening both greenhouses and once she had said goodbye and smiled and hugged them all again and smelled their oddly-identical musky grape heat, she was glad to be left alone. Friendly, yes – exhausting, certainly.

However welcoming they might be, she still did not feel like one of them. And she couldn't entirely decide if she wanted to be. Their happiness was tantalising. How fantastic it would be to have their peace, their confidence. But it wasn't something she thought she could have. Not really. Not ever.

She wished Matt were still here. His was the life, the openness, the freedom she had craved. Yet maybe the open road he travelled on was the road *most* travelled. And isn't it supposed to be better to take the road *less* travelled? Maybe Matt's road was too open, too wide open to easiness and emptiness and frothy nothingness.

Maybe he had offered her a bird's freedom – and a bird's freedom was not what she wanted, but a chosen path and a destination to aim for. If you set out with no paths to follow, won't you then just be the blown-along passenger of the wind and the tide and the stars, with no more power than a dandelion seed?

Wasn't there sometimes a time to choose? Maybe she would always have regretted being with Matt and his too-easy ways? Maybe his type of freedom would have held her back. Maybe his wasn't really freedom at all.

And then there was the waking dream. And her brother. And how the only place without shadows seemed to be the house on the hill.

She picked up the container of fertiliser and continued feeding the tomato plants, allowing herself to stop thinking and just to inhale the heat and smell and nature. She felt herself grow calm. And grow, not in size but in something else inside her. Almost as if in the greenhouses *everything* would grow and be bigger, better, riper than it could have been outside.

Soon she had fed all the tomato plants. No sign of David or the others. She looked through to the next greenhouse, the one with the peaches and grapes. Picking up her bag and the container of fertiliser, she went over to the door, which David had left slightly ajar, and pushed it open. She didn't know whether it could be opened from the inside and didn't want to risk it, so she propped it open with a small stick.

The heat in here was greater. For one wild moment Matilda wanted to take her clothes off. She grinned. That would shock them all! She pulled her T-shirt away from her skin and flapped the air over her stomach. Took a swig of water from the bottle in her bag. Sprinkled some of it over her face.

Matilda set to work. The heat grew and swelled but she knew she could get out at any time she chose, so she tantalised herself with the thought of fresh air, and continued working. Scoop, fill, pour, imagine the food reaching the roots, feeding, nourishing.

She reached up and took a peach from a low branch. It was too tempting to resist. Warm to the touch, still alive as she bit into it. Matilda thought that sweet peach was the most beautiful thing she had ever tasted. It was simply perfect. No words needed.

This could be the definition of happiness. Something you felt in your soul and had no need to explain. Something beyond language, beyond thought. Pure feeling and knowledge and rightness. Heaven.

She fed the plants some more and drifted into the silence that was her own. No one came to disturb her. It was as though she had been forgotten.

By the time she had finished feeding the plants in the second glasshouse, she was almost as hot as she could bear. But how she wanted to go into the last greenhouse! Those red flowers glowed through the steamy glass, the huge bloodiness of them weird and fascinating and magical. She would just go and look at them and smell them and *then* she would go and get some fresh air and cool down.

As she pushed open the door, which David had again left ajar, she stopped. She really was too hot. Almost dangerously so. Almost at that losing yourself stage when craziness takes over. No, she thought, I should go and get some fresh air first. That would be sensible. *Be careful – don't take risks*, she heard her mother's cautious voice buzz in her ear.

Was it supposed to be this hot? Surely no one could work in this? Had the cooling mechanisms failed again? She looked up at the vents. None was open. But it was only mid-morning. Perhaps the temperature wasn't at its maximum yet. She really didn't know.

She heard her mother's voice again. *You should have asked about that, Matilda. Always ask. Always be sure. Always better to be on the safe side.*

But the vast splashes of the bright-red flowers that she saw through the open doorway were irresistible. She pushed open the door fully, and it moved fast as if on a spring, so that a warm waft washed past her and the door swung towards the wall. She stepped in, ignoring her mother's voice, because you don't want to hear a mother's voice just before you do the one thing you really want to do.

And now it wasn't just the heat but the dripping smell. It took her breath away. She walked forward, dizzy with heat. Too much heat.

Yes, now she knew. This was a mistake. She had grasped one moment too many, had drunk one mouthful too much, had been greedy. She must get out and into the proper air and breathe again. She turned slowly round, fighting faintness, back towards the rebounding door.

And at that same moment, she heard its clunk as it swung shut.

Dived towards it, crashed against it with a painful thud, seeing shadows before her eyes as she fell. People? In the second greenhouse? But now she was on the ground, lying behind the door. They would not see her.

Blind with blood everywhere. In her chest, drowning her breath, choking the noise she needed to make. Her head was filled with thick scarlet, a pounding red across her eyes and in her ears. She closed her eyes. Or were they closed already? She floundered. Something was covering her head, something heavy and sweet-smelling and flowing over her face. She opened her eyes and saw red, red all over. She scrabbled at her face to get the cloying thing off. In her pounding dizziness, disappearing into a tunnel, she saw the flimsy scarlet flower flung aside from her, lying there grinning at her, its stamens like forked tongues.

No sound came from her mouth as she tried to scream again. And she slipped into the dark tunnelling water and disappeared.

# 2

## P is for Peace. Perfect Peace

Into her quiet dream came first the smell of strawberries, as he lifted her gently and lay her down on something soft and white. His hands barely touched her skin but she felt their cooling breath. Everything was white and shadowless, snowy cool on her forehead and her wrists and sometimes on the side of her neck. Water dripped into her mouth and slipped down her throat without her needing to swallow.

When he told her to sleep, she slept. Long and cool and peaceful and trusting.

He would look after her, the man with the long white robe and the Jesus hair and the golden light and the glow of right. And the words that seemed to flow from his fingers and to want to save her, protect her.

He would look after her, he would.

But when she woke later, she was confused. There had

been a man, the man, but when she opened her eyes there was only Maggie. Maggie, smiling.

'Hey, Matilda. You're awake!'

She tried to sit up but Maggie gently held her back.

'What happened? How . . . ?' She felt a sense of panic, of having been out of control. She was lying on a bed, in a room she didn't recognise.

'It's OK, Matilda. You got too hot. Heatstroke. We should never have left you for so long. But we thought if you got too hot you'd just come outside.'

'I tried . . . I tried . . .' She remembered the terrible fear when the door had closed.

'You should have propped the door open. But I'm afraid the thermostat stopped working again – it should never have been so hot in there. We're all so sorry – we feel terrible. When we found you lying there, we thought . . . Anyway, thank goodness you're all right! How do you feel?'

'Terrible headache. Funny, I didn't just now when I woke up. But now it's really . . .' She closed her eyes as the sudden pain swelled. Rubbed her temples hard. The pain only increased.

'I can get you something for that. Just hold on here for a few minutes and I'll be back. Don't try to get up, Matilda. Promise me?'

'Last thing I want to do,' Matilda slurred, wincing.

Maggie left the room and Matilda sank into the sounds of silence. Tried to focus on distant bird song and breeze, loosen the muscles in her face, ooze the pain away. She kept her eyes closed. The sunlight was too strong. The pain simply grew and spread until she wanted to cry with it.

Suddenly, Maggie was back. 'Matilda, I'm just going to lift your head and help you drink this. It's quite hot.' Matilda wanted to ask what it was but words would hurt. But as soon as she tasted it she knew. It was the passionflower and peach tea.

And as she floated away, she heard voices quiet and drifty, felt hands on her head, hands large and soft on each side of her face, strong and firm and anciently powerful, flowing through her like light. And the pain slowly went, breathed away by the man who stood silent behind her. She felt him and knew him but she could not open her eyes because, as he breathed out her pain, his breath was too heavy and she could not raise her eyelids.

It was the most intense and miraculous peace she had ever felt. Sun-soft, yellow and safe.

And as the voices quietly spoke around her, she ran towards her brother again, her brother with the Jesus hair and the white robe and no shadows anywhere around him. She ran laughing again through the warm rain towards him.

She nearly reached him. So nearly. When she woke there were no tears on her face at all. No rain falling anywhere.

# 3

# F is for Falling Faster, Further

Maggie drove Matilda back to the hostel the next morning. She had slept all the rest of the day before and in the evening someone had brought her food and a clean shirt and jeans which fitted her perfectly. She had tried to protest and say that she should get back to the hostel, but they would not listen and she did not press too hard. After all, it was comfortable and calm up here, and no one demanded anything of her, other than that she be happy. And that was wonderfully easy.

She did consider, briefly, what George would be thinking. It crossed her mind that he might be worried, but what could she do? And what did she care? He was a worrier. So, let him worry. He wasn't her problem.

Maggie blew her a kiss as she said goodbye at the front of the hostel. Everyone else was getting ready to go on the trucks to the field and it was impossible for Matilda to slink in unnoticed. She had expected looks from George, but why was everyone looking at her so oddly?

And then she realised. She was wearing a white shirt and pale blue jeans. Just like the people from the house. Blushing now, she hurried to her dormitory and changed into her normal clothes. Back outside again, she did her best to blend in amongst the others. It was not easy. Not because anyone was unfriendly, just because they seemed wary. Slightly silent. Almost as if she were one of the people from the house herself. George was the only one she knew well enough to talk to but he was the last person she wanted to talk to right then.

When the truck came to a halt and everyone piled off, she tried to latch on to their groups, tried not to be seen to be on her own, different. And she hoped that Rachel wouldn't single her out.

'Good morning, Matilda!' said Rachel brightly. 'How are you feeling now?'

'Fine, thanks, Rachel,' she replied politely. Just like the others. Trying not to meet Rachel's eyes.

'We were worried about you,' continued Rachel. 'But you look much better now. Tayberries today, section X. OK? Take care now. God bless.'

Was it her imagination or did Matilda sense a shrinking from the others? She looked away, muttered her thanks, and hurried towards the tayberry section. George soon caught up with her. By the time she had seen him, it was too late to avoid him. He said nothing, but silently handed her some containers and walked firmly beside her as they went towards the furthest row.

'Don't say anything, George, OK?'

'What? What was I going to say? What business is it of mine? Actually, I was going to ask if you were OK. I was worried when you didn't come back. I thought . . .'

'Oh, you're not going to go on about Jemima, are you? Look, nothing happened, OK?'

'Something happened, Matilda. Otherwise why did Rachel ask if you were OK? And why did you pitch up wearing their shirts and jeans? Christ, I thought you'd . . . I don't know what I thought, to be honest.'

'Nothing happened. I got too hot in the greenhouses, that's all – sort of fainted. Heat exhaustion. My fault – I could have left the greenhouses at any time but I didn't and then the door swung shut and I fainted. That's all. And they looked after me, let me sleep. Then it was too late to come back to the hostel, so I stayed. And my clothes were sweaty so someone lent me some. That's all. Nothing to get in a twist about.'

'Did you have any of that tea? Cake?'

'No,' she lied. George looked at her. 'No, George. Drop it. Nothing happened. Let's get picking, or we will have something to worry about.'

So they picked. And picked. And, in easier silence

now, they picked their way along the rows and through the morning. The dry sun beat hard on Matilda's shoulders and she felt the power of it ripening her.

Every now and then, she stopped to wipe the hair from her face and looked up towards the house on the hill, watched it throbbing in the haze. Once she saw him, the man with the robe and the Jesus hair. He walked slowly along the terrace, floating almost, followed by other figures, who could have been Maggie and David and Angel, but could have been anyone, really. And when he stopped and looked at her and she held her breath as she waited for the shadow to come and take her, nothing happened. No cold shadow rushing to envelop her. Only bright light shone from the house on the hill. And it smelled like heaven.

Later that day, in the afternoon, Matilda's job was pricing produce in the shop. George was somewhere else and Matilda was glad to be away from his caution and his worrying. She was working with Jules, the girl she had first met when she and Cally and Jack had arrived at the hostel.

Jules was silent. The silence grew too long. Matilda needed to break it.

'So, how long are you here for?' she asked.

'Till I get enough money together.'

'Oh, what are you saving for?'

'Uni.'

'Oh, right. Which one?'

'Too many questions. I'm not in the mood.'

Matilda looked up, startled at the tone of her voice. Jules was looking down, concentrating on weighing strawberries, her braids falling about her face, the beads knocking together each time she moved her head.

'Sorry,' Matilda muttered.

The silence hung over them now. Matilda could find no words in her head to break it.

Suddenly, Jules looked up, stopped what she was doing. 'Listen, I'm going to say this, ask this, whatever. Everyone wants to know.'

'What?'

'Why did you do that to Matt?'

'What do you mean? *What* did I do?'

'I heard – we heard – you told Them. About him taking drugs.'

'You're joking! That's ridiculous! Why would I do that? I liked him. I liked him a lot.'

'Yeah, that's what we heard too. You liked him a *hell* of a lot and he knocked you back. You pretended you didn't mind but then you told Them he had drugs. Very simple. Almost a cliché.'

'That's crap! There's no way I . . . Who's saying this,

anyway? This is just jealousy stuff, isn't it? Come on, who said it?'

'Everyone's saying it. And we think that's why They're being so nice to you now. Why you're getting special treatment. All this going up to the house and staying the night there. You're not the first to get sucked into that religious stuff, you know, and you won't be the last. And when you came back this morning wearing their clothes, I mean – Christ, you're almost one of them now!'

'Well, why not?' retorted Matilda, furious. 'Why shouldn't I? I mean, they're good to me, make me feel good. Not like the rest of you, all in your own selfish little worlds, not giving a toss what anyone else is feeling. I mean, barely no one here has asked me anything about myself, how I feel or anything.'

'This is a passing-through place, not a staying-and-pouring-out-your-life-story sort of place. It's somewhere you come for a while before you get on with real life. It's an unwritten rule – it's how it is. You weren't to know that but you didn't exactly try to pick it up, did you? You need to be a lot more sensitive to your environment, if you ask me.'

'Actually, I didn't ask you.'

'Fair enough,' said Jules reasonably, shrugging. After a short pause, she said, 'But where *did* Matt go? That's

174

what I want to know, and some of the others, too. He owed money to a couple of people. Including me. And I've been trying to phone his mobile.'

'You have his mobile number?' Matilda's heart leaped and overcame her anger.

'Yeah, course. Oh, right, so *you* don't?' Jules smiled.

'I'd only met him the day before, remember? And nothing happened like you said. And I didn't tell anyone about him taking drugs. I don't particularly care if you don't believe me.' And she didn't. 'But I'd really like to speak to him. We didn't say goodbye. Can I have his number? Please.' It hurt to say 'please' to this shoulder-shrugging don't-care girl, but there was no point in falling out with her if she had Matt's number.

'Won't do you any good. You just get the voicemail message.'

'He must have lost the phone or he's out of the country. Or he's run out of credit or whatever.' It would be something like that, thought Matilda. 'Can you let me have the number, though? Please? Just in case.'

Jules looked long at her. 'Yeah, OK. Maybe you didn't tell Them. Still think you shouldn't get too involved up at the house, though. If you want my advice.'

Which Matilda didn't, but she wasn't going to say

that right now. Jules pulled her own phone out of her bag, flicked through some numbers, wrote on a piece of paper and handed it to Matilda. Matilda looked at it and put it in her pocket.

They finished their work in near silence, commenting only on what they had between their hands, the piles of sweet fruit staining their fingers and every now and then one passing their lips.

F is for forbidden.

F is for fruit. And falling. Fast and far.

# 4

# I is for In

There was a note for Matilda on the noticeboard. George pointed it out to her as she walked though the front door of the hostel.

'Thanks, George.' She took it down and read it in the toilet.

> Dear Matilda
> We wondered if you'd like to come to supper on Saturday? If you're not doing anything else! It would be lovely if you could join us. We always have a special meal on Saturday and just relax. It'll be fun. Please come! Love, Maggie and David and the others xx
> PS We'll pick you up at 7 pm, if that's OK?

She knew immediately that she would go. She could

feel the cotton-wool warmth already. A fleeting doubt whispered that she should not, that other people would say she should not, that her parents would say she should not. But those were the people who made her feel bad. What was it Maggie had said, the first time she went to the greenhouse? Something about how you should spend time with people who care about you, who make you feel cared for. And you have to decide who those people are. Not Jules, who viewed this as a passing-through, don't-care, won't-question place, who had told her she needed to be more in tune with her environment, or something. Not boring George, who simply wanted her to follow rules. Or her parents, who simply wanted the safest-seeming route, the risk-free 'lie in bed in case the world falls on your head' route. Well, the world can fall on your head as you lie in bed, too. And if that happens, you get rubble all over your duvet too, she thought with a grin.

She screwed up the piece of paper and dropped it into the toilet, pulling the old-fashioned chain to flush it. It didn't work at first. The chain felt loose, not enough tug. She tugged again. Still no better. She looked up, tugged again. This time, the toilet flushed properly, but not before she noticed a piece of paper flutter to the floor. She picked it up. A torn-off corner from a roll-your-own cigarette paper.

Roll-your-own cigarettes made her think immediately of Matt and how he had not let her share his smoke. She looked at the paper again, turned it over. Just a cross, an X. That's all. A note that someone had written to someone else.

Of course, she could not help but briefly wonder about the mystery held in that cross. Who had written a note to someone and put it tucked into a toilet cistern? It could have been Matt, she realised. She had always thought, hoped, that he might have written her a note before he left. But there was no clue to follow and no way of ever knowing.

She put it in her pocket, along with the note of his phone number.

She tried the number as soon as she had a chance, finding a place where there was a signal. His voice was unbearably close. She almost smelled him. 'Hi! Matt here. Leave a message and I'll call you. Cheers!'

'Matt!' She said brightly, breathlessly. 'It's Matilda. Call me on this number. I need to know you're ok.' And she pressed the button to end the call, palms sweating, forgetting even to say goodbye. She looked at her phone. She took out the other scrap of paper and looked at them both. They could tell her nothing at all. She put them both in her pocket, for some kind of comfort, perhaps.

She spent the evening in front of the TV, bored but fixing her eyes to the screen. And then early to bed. It wasn't that people were unfriendly to her, but no one made any effort and she had lost the will to do anything herself. They had their friendships, their teams, their groups, sitting huddled and easy together. She could not intrude.

Lying in bed, she wondered at her alienation. Had she done it to herself? Was she difficult to know? Was she aloof? Cold? With Cally and Jack there, it had been easy, perhaps too easy. They had been like a shield. Now she needed that shield. She couldn't do it on her own.

But she had made friends easily with Matt, hadn't she? And the people at the house. They liked her. So the fault couldn't be with her. These were just unfriendly people. She was just unlucky that these were the first people she'd had to get along with since leaving school. They weren't like her. Didn't have the same things going on in their lives.

This was freedom and not all of it would be perfect, would it? She shouldn't expect that. She realised she *had* been expecting it and that was the problem. But what was wrong with dreaming? The best thing was to try to ignore or eliminate the parts of freedom that were not perfect and carry on dreaming, carry on hoping. Carry on moving towards the light.

Of course she would go to supper in the house on the hill. Because that was where the light was. It called to her, sucked her towards it on its breath. She smiled. Everything would be all right. It would.

# 5

# H is for Heaven on the Hill

As she walked into the room, following Maggie as she held the door wide for her, she *felt* the greeting, as if the world was smiling at her and folding her into it. David and Rachel came over to her. Hugged her. Rachel took her arm and pulled her over to a table with glasses of something sparkling.

'Here, take one of these. It's elderflower.'

Matilda sipped it, recognising the refreshing taste. She looked around. There were about twenty people. And others coming into the room. There were far more than she'd imagined. All looking similar, all clean. All the women with long, thick, untied hair; some of the men also with long hair. All with clean white shirts and pale jeans. Angel smiled at her and waved from the other side of the room. She looked for the man with the flowing robe but she didn't see him.

She let the chatter flow over her, joined in easily, fell back in the arms of their friendship. They asked no demanding questions, agreed with what she said, made her feel clever, and interesting, made her feel at one with them.

B is for belonging. And beautiful.

And brother and bed.

And bygones.

She had to turn round. She didn't know why. Something extra in the room. There he was, walking through the door. The man with the Jesus hair, followed by four women. He floated into the room and took each person's hand briefly. You could see them all smile as he did so. Occasionally he lingered and said a few sentences which she couldn't hear.

He was coming closer. She found her breath quickening. What would she say to him? Who was he? Why did she so want him to come to her and to touch her?

Slowly he approached, stopping tantalisingly often as he came. And now she could feel him near her, could feel the air change and swell and still, as if it held its breath. He walked behind her and she felt her eyes flicker and almost close as he passed behind her and to the other side of her. He spoke her name softly, *Matilda*, as though he had been waiting to meet her and say her name. And then, after a tiny, terrible pause he took her hand and she could barely breathe.

As he passed by and away from her, his words stayed behind in her ears, 'Good to see you again, Matilda. Lovely to see you again.' And she had said nothing in response, or nothing that she could hear, just something inside her.

After he had gone, she was aware of Maggie and David looking at her and smiling.

'Don't worry,' said Maggie. 'He always has that effect.'

And at that moment she knew what David had meant. Before. When he had said he would die for this man.

By the time they began to eat, sitting round a huge table, the mild elderflower wine had begun to go to her head. But she judged from the flushed faces and over-large smiles around her that everyone felt the same. She relaxed further. She was safe with these people. They were good people and they cared for her. It was obvious.

The chatter and the laughter curled themselves around her. She wished everyone could feel like this. If George was here now, and Jules, they would understand. Matt, too. He would love it here. He was wrong about them. She would try to text or phone him again later.

As the meal came to an end, Peter stood up. The

sounds washed away and everyone looked towards him. 'My friends,' he said. 'Fill your glasses and let us remember why we are here.' Four people came round, filling everyone's glass with a new drink. He smiled again, and his voice rose, sweet and warm like incense. 'Drink together, my friends, and then let the word of God into your heart.'

Matilda watched the others drink the contents of their glasses in one swallow, before she did the same. The liquid was thick and red, its taste powerful passionflower. She closed her eyes. And from that moment everything changed. She no longer needed to think about how to move her body. Something moved it for her. She no longer had to think what thoughts to think, what words to say. Her body was not hers. She had given it away.

The words wove in and out of her mind. She watched them come from his lips, saw them enter her heart and felt their meaning spreading inside her, to every distant cell.

'Let God arise, let His enemies be scattered: let them also that hate Him flee before Him. As smoke is driven away, so drive them away. Drive away His enemies with fire. The righteous cry and the Lord heareth and delivereth them, with fire into heaven. For only through fire shall they reach heaven. For the Lord loveth judgement and forsaketh not His saints; they are preserved for ever; but the seed of the wicked shall be cut off. The righteous shall inherit the land and dwell therein for ever. The mouth of the righteous speaketh wisdom. The law of God is in his heart and none of his steps shall slide.'

Matilda swayed at the strange words, eyes closed, and drank them in, knowing their meaning fully. She felt hands in hers, strong hands holding her. Felt His words come close, His breath behind her, felt her heart fly and soar like a spirit as He lifted her to Him. White shadows danced all around her and inside her and through her and the shadows were like watery laughter.

S is for shadows.

And soul.

And saved.

She woke in the morning in the bed where she had woken that other morning. The window was wide open and a breeze blew the curtains inwards. Last night seemed like a dream. It had been as though she was drunk, and yet she knew she hadn't been. And this morning she felt clear and light and rinsed through. And happy. Not a shadow anywhere.

It was as though, last night, someone else had been inside her body, guiding it.

The door opened and in came Maggie. 'Good morning, Matilda. How are you today?'

'Good, thanks, Maggie. You?'

'Yes, good, thanks. Time you got up, though. And do come again next week. Consider yourself invited. Just let one of us know. Now, David will run you back when you're ready.'

She hadn't really thought about going back. She wished she could stay. She hesitated.

'Maggie? Can I ask you something?'

'Sure.'

'If I wanted to stay. I mean, for ever. Like you and the others. I mean, how could I do that?'

Maggie's eyes lit up. 'Oh! Well, you'd have to want it, I mean really want it. And you have a family. You'd have to cut yourself off from them – that's hard Matilda, very hard.'

'I could do that,' she found herself saying. 'They don't need me, anyway. I just worry them and annoy them.'

'You need to think about it. Properly. It's not something you can just decide. We wouldn't want you to do something you didn't really feel in your heart.'

'I do! I know this is what I want. Anyway, if I don't like it after a while, if I change my mind, I can leave, can't I?'

Maggie looked straight at her. 'Sure, you can leave. Any time you want.'

'Well, tell me what I have to do. I really want this.' And she did. Anything was better than feeling like an outsider with too many choices and no signposts.

'How much do you remember of last night, Matilda?'

'All of it. It *was* quite hazy but I remember all of it.'

But soon, when Maggie had gone and Matilda was getting dressed, she wondered whether she *had* remembered all of it. Surely what she remembered – the floating, the hands, the words – hadn't taken all night? And how had she got to her bed?

She frowned and tried to remember the rest. A cross. There was a cross! That was it! How could she have forgotten? And he, Peter, had stood on the cross and someone had . . . no, that couldn't be right. Not nails? Surely ropes. Yes, ropes, that was right. And they had all stood and held their arms towards him. And there had been a bowl of fire somewhere. At some point they had been chanting something, all of them, Matilda too. What had they been chanting?

She tried to think. She felt it was something so obvious that she couldn't decipher it from the rest of the obvious thoughts in her head. It wasn't significant. It was just something very ordinary.

*I will die for you, Lord*. That was it. Well, obviously she

189

would die for Him. What was so strange about that? You would do that for anyone you loved, wouldn't you? She would go through fire for Him.

At that moment, she looked at her bare feet. She didn't know why she looked. There was a red mark on each of them, just on the top, in the middle. Sitting on the edge of her bed, she looked underneath her foot. Both feet. There were marks there, too. She touched the marks. She felt nothing at all. But they looked like burns. They looked exactly like burns.

# 6

## P is for Peach-perfect

Early August. The height of the harvest season, the plants heavy with fruit, swaying sluggishly, slow and drooping, oozing sap, wasps swimming drunkenly. A humming summer, brimful.

For the next few days, Matilda floated. Now that she knew that she wanted to be with the people in the house on the hill, she cared little about the distance between her and the other workers. She didn't need them.

There had been no reply from Matt. She had left another message. And a text. But there were plenty of possible explanations. And nothing she could do.

One day, at lunchtime, sitting in the shade of a tree, happily on her own, she heard someone approach. She turned. George. He sat down next to her. How young he seemed now. How silly and vulnerable. Poor George. How much she could teach him.

'Hi,' he said.

'Hi,' she replied, with her eyes shut.

'You OK?'

'Yes. You?'

'You've changed.'

'Oh?' Still with her eyes shut. Not caring what he meant. Poor silly George.

'See?'

'No. What do you mean?'

'See – before, you would have bitten my head off for saying you had changed.'

'I don't think so. Anyway, that's good, isn't it? I mean, that I didn't bite your head off?' She opened her eyes.

'Yeah, definitely,' said George. He looked at her. 'What happened on Saturday night?'

'Just a nice meal. Nice company, nice chat, nice evening.'

'I'm worried about you. It's just like with Jemima. She changed, just like you're doing. She always said nothing was going on.'

'Nothing's going on, George. Apart from you. You're going on and on. Don't be such a worrier.' She lay back. A faded part of her knew that she *was* different. But it was a difference she liked. It was ripe and soft and peach-perfect and round. It was natural. What was wrong with changing? She had wanted to, hadn't she?

192

To be different? To grow into herself? Maybe she was doing exactly that, just faster than most people. That was good too. How could she have thought she wanted what Matt had offered her?

She wanted to tell George, to share her happiness with him. Could he not understand her need for this, for beauty and mystery and belief and belonging?

'I'm happy there, George, up there in the house. It's like what home should feel like. Everything I want is there.'

'You'll be saying God is there next.'

She closed her eyes again. 'God is there, George. Of course He is.'

Saying it was like flying. Like cutting through the ropes. She smiled inside. If this was what made her feel like flying, then this was what she would have.

When she opened her eyes, George had gone. She took her shoes and socks off and touched the fading red marks on her feet.

George would not understand. Could not. He had not been saved. This was what it felt like, being saved. Like being pulled back from the edge. Or being pushed over and caught before hitting the ground. Or falling upwards. And more than all those.

Another faded part of her distantly remembered how she had wanted to mock the people at the house when they spoke like this, when they talked of God, and how she had even cringed. But now she was saved. Simple. Like faith. Ask no questions. If you have faith you don't need to question. Just let go. Fall over the edge and He will save you.

Next time Matilda spoke to George, it was too late.

# 7

## L is for Letting Go. And Lost

As the days passed and summer ripened, fruit matured fast and was picked before it could burst, the earth warmed and, in the greenhouses, the scarlet passionflowers swelled and bloomed and grew to extraordinary sizes, slowly dropping their nectar.

The August heat increased, the air thickened, heads ached, breathing slowed. No one could remember a summer like it. It had rained, enough for the fruit, but only at night, so it passed almost unnoticed.

Matilda could feel something else. A difference amongst the people at the house. Oh, they still smiled, still floated, still breathed out warmth to her, still held everyone else in their long gaze. They still had the same power.

But they were somehow quieter. Somehow closer to each other. Holding something inside. And occasionally, when some of them looked at Matilda, it was as though they knew something she didn't. Perhaps they were wondering whether she was with them. She wanted to be with them. She wished she could show them that, crush their doubts, prove herself to them so they would take her for ever.

Sometimes she would catch one of them just standing staring into space, gazing up the hill at the house, as if in a trance. One day, Thursday, she saw Angel doing this. Matilda walked up to her and called her quietly from behind, but Angel didn't hear. Matilda touched her softly on the shoulder and Angel leaped round, a rabbit-frightened shock on her face. Then she relaxed, 'Oh, Matilda, sorry – you made me jump.'

'You seemed far away,' said Matilda.

'Yes, yes. Yes,' said Angel again, pressing her fingers to her forehead.

'Are you all right?' asked Matilda.

'Oh, absolutely. Absolutely. But listen . . .' And then she turned away.

'What?'

'No, nothing, nothing,' said Angel, smiling desperately now. 'Nothing.'

'Maggie asked me if I was coming on Saturday again,' said Matilda. 'Can you say that I'd love to? I had such a good time last week.'

'No!' said Angel loudly, oddly.

'Sorry?'

Angel's words tumbled over each other. 'No, I mean, of course, but . . . Well, you know, Matilda, you have to think about this really hard, you know. I mean, I know Maggie said you could join us, but do you really want to cut yourself off like this? I mean, what about your family? What will they think?'

Angel's face was white. Her hands moved like damaged birds.

'What's wrong, Angel? You look . . . Are you OK?'

'I'm fine. I'm fine.' She looked around, wildly. 'Sorry, I've got to go.' And she rushed away, down the track to the car park. A few seconds later, Matilda heard the sound of a vehicle and soon saw the silver roof of the car speeding up the lane towards the house on the hill.

Friday. Friday morning, a thin fog veiling the hills as she climbed on to the truck to go up to the fields. A cooler day, a welcome greyness in the air.

Her name, shouted from a distance. She turned. David. Calling from the car park at the front of the hostel.

Her heart leaped. She jumped down from the truck. He hurried towards her. 'Hi, Matilda. We need you up at the house today. You OK for that?'

'Yeah, sure,' she said, buttery warmth spreading through her. She ignored any looks the others might be throwing at each other. Ignored George and whatever he might be thinking. Almost ran towards David and sang inside herself as the car bounced up the potholed lane towards the house.

And now in the greenhouse, the heat again, even without the sun, familiar, pillow-soft. Tempranillo heat. The tomato taste, the plants perspiring into the moist and silent air.

'So, what today?' she asked.

'Picking today,' he replied. 'And then we'll see. You OK for tomorrow night?' he asked as he handed her a pile of stacked containers, and they started to work.

'Yeah, I told Angel.'

'Oh, right.' Something in his voice, a tiny hesitation?

'Is she OK? She seemed, I don't know – well, we had a bit of an odd conversation yesterday.'

'She's fine. But how are you?' he continued quickly.

'Good.'

'Yeah, you look great, Matilda. You know? There's something . . . well, you're glowing, is all I can say.' He stopped picking and turned to look at her. Now, when he looked at her, she simply loved his warmth and nothing more. No gut-crushing feeling, just the smile inside.

'I feel great, David. I just love being here. I feel . . . cared for. You've all been so kind to me. I was quite . . .' She hesitated. 'I was quite unhappy, you know? I didn't know what I wanted.'

'What changed?'

'I did. Something here is changing me. I had something hanging over me, like a weight, a shadow, but each time I've been here, the shadow's gone further and further away, got fainter and fainter. I can even believe it will go completely, one day. If I stay here.'

'Your brother.'

'Yes, my brother.' So simple, just to say it. Her brother. Hers. He *had* belonged to her. It was her parents who had taken him away from her by shutting her out of his illness and his death. And only here, at the house on the hill, in Heaven, was she able to know that; only here would she be able to meet her brother, one day, and to ask his forgiveness. Forgiveness for not running to him when he called her before. For not loving him. For being jealous of a boy who suffered so much before he died.

And she had nearly reached him.

She smiled at David, turning to him again as she picked a truss of tiny orange tomatoes. 'My brother.'

And he smiled back and she knew she was where she

199

belonged. Here she could be happy for the rest of her life.

Soon, Maggie and another girl came into the greenhouse. Matilda was introduced to the other girl, Cara. Cara smiled, held out her hand. 'I've heard all about you,' she said. 'And I hear you are going to stay with us? That's wonderful.'

So it was decided? Matilda sang inside. They had accepted her. It was as easy as that. No more talk of whether it was the right thing or not. Everyone simply knew it was.

'Would you two like some tea, cake?' Maggie asked.

'Yep, course we would, wouldn't we, Matilda?'

The four of them walked out into the clear air and round to the front of the house. And as before, Matilda sat down, relaxed, drank, relaxed some more and closed her eyes as willingly as always, hungrily drinking in the feeling she knew would come and which she needed.

Into her waking dream she drifted until she was outside the house again, the passion-red smell of fire and dying seeping from the ancient walls. She walked eagerly up to the house on the hill. Here was the window and through it a new scene: no man and no woman beside the bed, no one dressed in best clothes, no one beautiful and shining and privileged. No one weeping by the bed of a son. Matilda looked at the bed and was not surprised to see no boy in the bed. Her brother was not there.

In her half-dream, she turned and looked, up the hill which now stretched further upwards into the sky. And she knew now that she could look in any direction she wanted. Because he would always be there. Because he always was. And when she did, she saw him there, at the top of the hill, by the house. Calling her. Her brother, with golden Jesus hair and a white robe and sandals.

'Come with me, Matilda. It is time. Time to go. Come on, Matilda.' And she ran towards him now, running up the hill again towards what she saw there. In her dream she did run towards her brother.

And in her dream now she reached him. At last, she reached her brother and there was no warm rain running down her cheeks, no rain at all in heaven.

No one woke her gently before she reached the top. No one woke her while she wrote a letter to her parents. No one woke her while she signed it. No one woke her while someone took her mobile phone from her bag.

She let them carry her into the house. She let them undress her. She let them dress her again. In pale blue jeans and white shirt. She let them brush her hair. And bless her and seal her lips with blood–red passionflower nectar to steal her soul.

This was her family now. She would stay with them until the end.

P is for perfect.

*Part Five*

**The Year 2029**

# Prison – One Week
## Before Release

How strong you had to be, how strong, to do this work. To stay on the road never travelled. So thought the little old woman as she eased her weathered Branson Mirage to a halt in front of the prison walls. She leaned back in the faded squishtic seat and gently stroked the steering wheel, remembering all they had been through together, and all that they still had to do. She was tired, she was, the little old woman with slow bones and battered spirit.

It was damaging work on the edge of hell.

She unfolded her legs somewhat creakily from the low seat and climbed out of the car. She stood for a moment and looked up to the many-eyed walls, the walls that held so much sadness, badness, madness – no, she really did not care. She was here to do her duty. To save this one soul. And herself.

And then, tightening her eyes, hardening her jaw, firming her heart one last time, the little old woman walked slowly towards the entrance. Soon, for the very last time, she was entering those raw liver walls, passing her knobbly fingers over the security scanner, staring innocent-eyed at the iris-recognition system. One last time, the falsely welcoming voice spoke: 'Good afternoon, Mrs Bailey. Come through, please,' and the door swished open into somewhere. Then, after a few automatic words with the bored young man in the Control Centre, and an unknowing wave from several of the pastel-suited Rehab officers, and a hopeless stroke of the Facilitator's cat, she was on her way, following the young female Rehab officer – young enough to be her granddaughter – along the familiar, calming corridors.

Not that she had a granddaughter. Of course. Nor ever would.

As the door opened in front of her, her heart gnarled and her breath split in her chest and she struggled not to hurl herself at him in her hatred. Because, tired as she was, her hatred for what he had done would never fade. It was this hatred which allowed her to continue to fight for his soul. She had dedicated her life to this, she had. With passion.

She smiled at him. Somehow, she smiled as he came towards her with his silly hair and his soft blue eyes.

'Good afternoon, Peter. How are you today?'

He murmured a reply as he held out his hands towards her, although of course they did not touch. Her stomach shifted as he smiled at her. She looked down, as if shy, though shy she was not. Just careful.

A Rehab officer brought them some tea. Around his thin white neck, he wore a necklace of twisted blue lines, a blue cross hanging from it. When he had put the tray down, he brushed his floppy hair from his forehead and she saw a tiny tattoo on his temple, an electric-blue cross. Her mouth twisted in an almost imperceptible smile. Fashion or faith? She would have liked to ask him. Did he know? Had he thought? Had he asked the right questions or had he just let himself fall blindly into whatever comforting arms were offered?

'Here you are, Mrs B,' he said. 'Will you be Mother?'

'Aren't I always?' she replied. Proper cups this time, she noticed. Peter was being allowed proper china cups for this visit. A week before release and an inmate must be trusted not to smash the china and cut his visitor's throat with a jagged edge. Otherwise, release would be unwise. The evil must be sucked out before the inmate is freed.

And when the Rehab officer had left the room and gone to his position behind the glass, and the metallic smell of stewed prison tea filled the space between her and Peter, she spoke. But first she reminded herself that she must resist his powers. She would stay strong, she would, she *would*, this steely, little old woman with her dusty skin and oh-so-tired heart.

'Well, Peter, how are you feeling? Only one week to go now. You must be excited. Nervous, I should imagine? Perhaps more than a little nervous?'

'I feel quite calm really, Sarah, strangely calm. Thanks to you. You have helped me so much. I cannot tell you how much.' He rubbed his side, as if something was hurting him there.

'Oh, don't be silly. I have done nothing. If God has forgiven you, it is not because of me. It is between you and God. I simply come here and drink tea with you.'

'Oh no! You underestimate yourself. You have been more help than you imagine. And I have something for you, to say thank you.' Peter turned and gestured to the Rehab officer through the glass and the man stood up as though he had been waiting for this, and came through, carrying something. Something which he held carefully, of peculiar shape, roughly covered by newspaper.

'Close your eyes, Sarah.'

She looked at the Rehab officer. Surely she should not close her eyes? Close her eyes with a convicted mass murderer only a few feet from her?

'It's OK, Mrs Bailey. The Facilitator has given permission,' said the Rehab officer, his pale indoor skin slightly shiny and oddly naked in the bright shadowless light. Above his head, the blue square of the high-up window looked down on her. Freedom was out there. Everything was possible in the blank square piece of sky.

'I don't like surprises. I don't want to shut my eyes,' she said, feeling silly, irritated, vulnerable.

'Please, Sarah. It is a surprise, a present for you,' said Peter, that voice turning her stomach. How could anyone fall for his cloying milkshake fakery?

She closed her eyes. There was no way out. She must play along with him, pretend to be the weak little old woman he thought she was. It was the only way to carry through her intentions.

She had promised God that He would decide. She kept that thought rigid in her mind, quelling any others, any more secret and dangerous thoughts. What *would* God decide, she wondered? *Had* Peter had done enough? How *could* God forgive him? Surely Peter must pay more, pay properly? Surely a just God would want that?

She fingered her loose rings.

She heard a rustling. Heard soft-soled footsteps walk away. 'Can I open my eyes, now?'

After a tiny pause, Peter's voice: 'Now, Sarah, open your eyes now.'

When she did, she had to gasp. Flowers, bursting

from the ragged string which bound their waists, spraying every shade of red across her eyes. Standing in a jam-jar. Hanging fuschia, furled sweet peas, rich fat roses, sweet sleepy poppies, and in the middle a beautiful blood-coloured flower, enormous, the size of her two hands. Its five stamens pointed towards her, a tiny drip at the end of one, a diamond drip of silvery liquid, like glycerine. Hanging there, waiting to drop.

She watched it, her eyes wide. Wanted to nudge it to make it drop. She moved her teacup. Sipped a little.

'Well? What do you think, Sarah? I grew them in my garden. I grew these for you.'

'What is it? The one in the middle?' She knew what it was, but she knew she could not tell him. Never had she seen one so perfect. She couldn't take her eyes off it, its huge bloody throat, the stamens like eyes. The teardrop growing, still waiting to fall. If she even breathed too hard, surely it would fall. Her lips felt dry. She moistened them with her tongue, raised a finger to smooth the ridge of crusty lipstick she felt there. Wiped away the old woman spittle from the corners of her mouth.

'Ah, yes, I thought you'd like that one. That, Sarah, is a very special flower. It's a passionflower, but a very unusual strain. Do you know about the passionflower?'

'*Passiflora*, hundreds of species, many different colours

210

and behaviours. Some medicinal uses. Calming, I think. That's all. I have grown one or two,' she said, vaguely.

'Nothing like this one, I expect?'

'No, nothing like this one, Peter. It's ... extraordinary.' She stared.

Peter stroked his finger round the flower's lips as he spoke. She held her breath, waiting for the nectar to fall. Now all of the stamens held a drip on their tips, too. All waiting for the moment to fall. His words were marshmallow soft.

'The passionflower represents aspects of the Crucifixion. You see, Sarah, there are five petals and five sepals, representing the ten disciples, minus Judas and Peter, of course. You know why Peter was excluded, don't you?' She nodded. Of course she knew. He did not need to patronise her. Peter – this Peter – continued. 'Here, see – we have the outer fringe, representing the crown of thorns.' His other hand touched his forehead absently, before he continued again. 'And here, this is called the pistil – and these bits sticking out are the stigmata, and look like the nails which pierced our Lord on the cross. Finally, of course, the five stamens represent the number of wounds Christ received. And see – see, Sarah – how they bleed.'

She watched. But it was not blood. It was nectar, just nectar oozing naturally from a flower. She watched as he shook the plant slightly and the drops of liquid flew off, landing scattered on the table.

But she had forgotten her manners. 'Peter, thank you,' she said, seeming flustered. 'Thank you very much. You should not have gone to such trouble.'

'I have something else,' said Peter. And from behind the flowers, where it had been hidden, he pushed a small cardboard container covered with a white handkerchief. She looked at the Rehab officer through the glass. He nodded back at her with a grin. He knew about this. She felt trapped.

Peter was beginning to manipulate her again, he was. She would not let him. Not now, not so close to the end.

And now when she looked at him with his buttery eyelashes and his misty hair and his lips the colour of crushed raspberry, she could not stop the uncoiling of her hatred. And her deep and secret distrust of God. Because if God could forgive this, him, and what he had done, then did God deserve Peter's soul at all? How *could* God forgive what he had done? A good God could not.

She must crush such thoughts or God would hear.

She could smell the passionflower, its sweet heady sleepy smell drifting around the room. It was a beautiful scent, it was.

Out of the corner of her eye she saw . . . snapped her gaze away, looked back again. No, it was normal, quite normal. She had thought for a moment, one silly, fuzzy moment, that the nectar oozing from the palms of Christ's hands, the stamens, was red. But it was only the reflection of the huge red petals cloaking it. How silly she had been! The strain was getting to her. She must keep control.

'Go on, uncover them,' urged Peter, pointing towards the cardboard container. The little old woman stretched out her hands and hesitantly removed the cloth. Tiny strawberries glistened there, with miniature green leaves like cuffs gently cupping them.

It was all she could do not to throw them in his face. Strawberries! Did he not know? Did he not realise what he had done with his strawberry fields and his empty dreams of heaven and his lying promises to the poor young people who had suffered there? Did he not remember how many people had died, sliced to pieces by flying glass and their skin burned off by sheets of fire? Had he no remorse?

The stench of burnt fruit came to her and she held her throat tight closed.

And then she remembered, if she had briefly forgotten before, why she was there.

So she managed to hold her hate inside. She smiled at

213

him with her wrinkled lizard-eyes, and he thought the moisture there was merely a softening in her. As he pushed the box towards her and she reached out her gnarled fingers like branches to receive them, he looked at the diamonds on her hands and thought deep inside himself, *I hate you old woman, with your riches and your greedy silent taking of my fruit.*

And as she took the strawberries to her and stared at them, drinking in their long-gone summer scent, the thought she held inside her was, *I hate you, I do, evil man with your stupid Jesus hair. I hate you because you gave me strawberries and did not understand what they meant.*

'Thank you, Peter,' she said, 'It was very kind of you.'

'It was nothing. I grow things for the glory of God. I always have. I kept it a secret, to surprise you. I didn't tell you I was growing strawberries. But tell me, did you, I wonder . . . I hardly know how to ask . . .'

'Yes, Peter, what?'

'Well, do you remember last week, we talked about something? I said I'd had an idea, for how to repay my debt.'

She held his gaze. 'Yes, I do vaguely recall something, Peter. Tell me again.' She would make him sweat, she would, the not-so-fragile old woman with a will of her own and secret thoughts inside her which he would never find.

'Well,' said Peter, rubbing his side again, his eyes narrowing briefly with pain, 'my idea about making a place where children could go for holidays. Children who suffer, so that they could have some joy, something to lighten their lives. Some children suffer so much. I suffered, you know, and I've told you some of it. And now all I want is to pay something back. God will stay with me if I do that, Sarah. And I am so frightened about God leaving me. That He will desert me again and allow me to be deceived.'

'And remind me how you think I could help, Peter. I'm just an old woman. I am just a Volunteer Friend, just doing my bit. That's all.'

He looked at her, rubbing his side still. 'Oh no, you are so much more than that. I see so much more in you. True goodness. You are truly God's child. And you have so much more to give.'

'I have nothing to give, Peter. I am tired and old.'

'You and I together, Sarah. Would you like some more tea?'

'Yes, please. Thank you.' She watched his slow fingers wrap softly around the teapot and there was silence between them as the steaming tea fell into her cup and then into his. As he put the pot down, the edge

215

caught on a teaspoon and the spoon flicked into the air and clattered onto the floor, falling on her side of the table.

She bent down to pick it up. As she straightened up again, she felt the blood rush back to her head, dizzying her briefly. Low blood pressure. She knew that – her newly-installed Compudoc had diagnosed it and even given her a little print-out saying, in simple language, that it was nothing to worry about. And when she had made a fuss and managed to get an appointment with an actual doctor, he had confirmed it: 'You don't die of low blood pressure, he'd said. You might feel dizzy but you don't die of it.' So she had taken little notice of her recent increasing bouts of dizziness, her tiredness, her occasional lack of balance. Low blood pressure, she had told herself. Nothing to worry about. The Compudoc was a reliable system. Sometimes better than a real doctor, the adverts said.

It took a few seconds for the dizziness to fade. The passionflower swayed slightly. Peter watched her, concern in his face. 'Are you all right, Sarah?'

He saw the diamonds squatting on her twig-like fingers. How greedy, how ugly, he thought. His mother would have had something to say about such riches.

'Yes, I'm quite fine,' she replied, drinking her strong

tea, now more stewed than ever. But deliciously sweet, a little sweeter than she usually allowed herself.

'I put sugar in for you, Sarah. I hope I put the right amount in?'

She smiled, pausing and looking directly into his eyes. 'Yes, thank you, Peter, it is perfect. You were saying?' she said. She couldn't remember what he was saying but it was something. Something . . .

His words jumbled into her head. The dizziness really wasn't passing. She struggled to focus on what he was saying. 'And then we could see . . . together we would help . . . God's work . . . fruits of fire . . .'

And she was speaking too, her words mixed up in what he was saying and that mixed up with what she was thinking. She knew she was saying things and she knew exactly what they were – and why – because she was still in control, she was, she knew she was, and she loved the familiar dizziness and the floating away free and oh, her heart now so strangely aching and crackling pain across her chest and falling flying hands large strong hands feather soft fingers across her forehead under her arms and words tumbling away from her as the breath of him flowed over her and took her away to a white space.

It must have been only a few seconds before the tired old woman found herself sitting at the table with her head in her hands.

And Peter looking at her, talking. 'Are you all right, Sarah?'

'What? Oh, how silly of me! Just a dizzy spell. I am quite all right. It's just a little low blood pressure. What were you saying?'

Peter smiled, 'No, Sarah, *you* were saying. About helping me, when I get out.'

'Oh yes, of course, so I was.'

'Thank you, Sarah. Thank you from the bottom of my heart. For everything. You cannot know how much you have done. You have saved me, you know.'

'Oh, it was nothing, Peter. I have told you before, nothing.'

How tired she felt now. She must hold on. She pressed her fingers to her forehead. Brought her hands back to the table, noticed the ridged nails, a little too long, not quite so perfectly shaped now. She must not let herself go, she mustn't, with her neat tailored outline, her perfect crisp hair, her chic handbag from Bond Street and elegant shoes below her tidily tapering ankles. And her tired heart aching with thoughts too deep for him to reach. Too deep for anyone to know.

'To be able to help God's children, Sarah, it's all I ask. To give them what I never had. I have told you part of my suffering. I need to tell you the rest. You have no children but I know you understand.' She shrank inside

218

as he continued. 'It helps so much, to be able to tell you. I have told the doctors, of course, but they don't listen with their hearts. You do. I know you do, and it helps me so much.'

She waited for the story which was to come. For the test of her strength. She waited for him to try to manipulate her, to make her see his suffering so that she would think he deserved to be forgiven. She knew what he was trying to do. He thought he deserved forgiveness. It was his way of begging. And resisting his begging was her way of proving that she was stronger than him. Her heart began to race, in anticipation of the test. And in anticipation of watching him suffer again.

She watched his flat fingers fluttering above the table, saw through his Jesus hair, noticed his eyelashes veiling his pale blue eyes, and she waited.

He drew in a deep breath, pressed one hand into the side of his abdomen, and began to speak.

And as he spoke, the nectarine words dropping from his lips, she could picture the scene exactly.

*The boy, eleven years old, stood in the noonday glare, smelling the African sun roasting his hair, feeling his skin shrivel under the crackling heat. His hands stung badly, scratched to pieces by the thorns. But it was his fault. He should never have picked the roses, should never have ripped them from their natural* places. The fact that it was for his mother's birthday only made it worse. She did not deserve such a bad boy. A boy who ripped his hands to shreds on her precious roses, cultivated from stock she had brought from England when God had called them to be missionaries. A thieving boy who had not learned right from wrong.

She was good. His mother was good and pure. He should never have picked her beloved roses. Honour thy father and mother. Thou shalt not steal their roses.

His mother and father had given their lives to helping people, saving their souls from godlessness and bringing them to heaven. They had failed to save their own son's soul. He had made them grieve. His mother grew extraordinary fruits and flowers in her Tanzanian garden, all for God's glory, watering them daily, drawing them up with her hands, and her son was sent by the Devil to uproot her work.

So now he was standing here in the crazying cicada-heat, his skin searing. Naked. His lips cracking and drying. Deserving punishment.

The boy looked through dizzy eyes towards the house, looked at the cool, dark doorway where his parents stood. His mother clasped her hands around a bowl. His father carried a stick.

He stood there still, the boy, tall and strong and ready now. On the hot stones he must stand and he must close his eyes and pray as his feet burned. He forced himself to pray, and not to *think about the lethal heat and his parents watching him from the house. He swayed and prayed, as they had taught him. If he prayed hard enough he would be forgiven.*

*He could pray hard enough. He could. Now he could.*

*He did not hear his parents walk towards him. He carried on praying. Beautifully he prayed and high flew his soul.*

*Now the mother and father were there and the son held his arms away from his body for what must come. He heard the noises of sticks being broken, piled, stacked. Heard the rasp of the match, smelled the crackle of the flames as they began to flicker, felt the heat as they licked the air by his feet. And then he heard the stillness as the mother and father waited and prayed.*

*Soon he felt the terrible pain as the red-hot stick was held against his side and pressed onto his flesh lovingly and hard, harder still. He heard his skin sizzle as the stick seared his body. He breathed over the pain and prayed through it.*

*As the boy parted his lips, the father held a sponge to his mouth on the end of a stick and, gratefully, the son pressed his lips on the sponge and sucked the passionflower sweetness from it.*

*Joy flowed down his face. And at last he met God and God took away his pain and forgave him, because he had prayed well.*

*Then the mother and the father knelt and prayed with their son. For their son. And their son prayed with them. For them.*

*Fire-like pain shot through their knees, but still the mother and father prayed. Their muscles went into spasm against the baking stones, but they did not stop praying. Their fingers and bare toes arched with cramp, but still they never stopped loving their only son and praying with him. And at last their prayers had been answered.*

*God had taken their son. He had accepted him.*

Peter lay back on his bed and relaxed. A satisfied smile spread over his face. He had won! The silly old woman, greedy for God's love, had succumbed to his powers. Such a small amount of *Passiflora sacrisanguinarium*, that was all it had taken, the silly, weak old bag, the ugly wrinkled bitch, rich witch. The love of money is the root of all evil. How true are God's words.

He remembered the words of God, spoken to him so often as he had learned to pray.

'For all flesh is as grass. And all the glory of man is as the flower of grass. The grass withereth and the flower thereof falleth away. But the word of the Lord endureth for ever. Better is the end of a thing than the beginning thereof. In my end is my beginning. In my end is my beginning, Lord. The day of death is better than the day of birth.'

And Peter knew that with the little old woman's help he could bring many more people to a new beginning. In their end was their beginning. He did it only for their salvation, to save their souls and bring them to God.

He would do it again. He would do God's will. He never doubted it.

'One generation passeth away and another generation cometh. And the fire never sayeth, enough.'

The fire never has enough. Peter would *never* finish saving souls for God.

The little old woman sped from the prison grounds in her battered red Mirage, its roof back, the wind in her once-tidy hair. She gripped the steering-wheel tightly, her fingers pressed deep into the forgiving squishtic surface, the sinews of her worn hands protruding wire-like, her jaw clenched. Half a mile later, she breathed at last and slowed the car to a halt.

She flung open her door, climbed out and steadied herself briefly, before hurrying round to the other side, where she reached over and picked up the bunch of flowers and the box of strawberries. She positioned them carefully in front of the car, on the ground. Walking back to the driver's side, she climbed in, tickled the engine to a quiet start and reversed a few yards until she could see the red splashes on the road before her. She paused, gunned the engine to a screaming roar, and deftly slid her foot from the clutch at the same time as pressing down on the accelerator.

Some time later another car would pass and another driver would wonder why the road was strewn with blood-red flowers and strawberries, a bizarre massacre on a quiet Devon road.

As she drove at speed along the lanes towards her home, the little old woman fought the dizziness that threatened again to overcome her.

It had been a terrible story. A terrible and horrible story. Beautiful in its way, too, very beautiful. And now, at last, it was enough.

She had heard enough. His soul would be saved. But for her. Not for God.

To this she would dedicate her remaining life. As she had always intended.

She smiled as the wind washed through her loosened hair. She laughed at the taste of passionflower on her tongue. She hugged to herself the knowledge that she had won. Did he think he could trick her like that? Did he really think she didn't know about the rare, so rare, *Passiflora sacrisanguinarium*? That she hadn't grown it herself every year for the last twenty-five years, each year stronger, bloodier. Each year more powerful. Did he not know that she was as immune to its powers as he was? That she loved to sink into the peace it offered but that it never had the power to twist her thoughts or her will.

She knew what he had done with *Passiflora sacrisanguinarium*, all those years ago.

The dizziness that had overcome her briefly in the prison had only stemmed from her tiredness, her slowing heart, not the passionflower juice he had put in her tea when he thought she wasn't aware. And it was the same slight dizziness she felt still. The Compudoc had said she shouldn't be driving on her own. But what did a computer know? And what did she care?

As she pulled towards a halt outside her ancient rambling-rosey cottage, the chintz curtains twitched and a face disappeared from the window. She opened the glove compartment and took out a small dark blue bottle. She unscrewed the lid, held the mouth beneath her nose and inhaled deeply. She put her finger over the lips of the bottle and tipped it over and back again, leaving a shining red globule on her finger. Closing her eyes, she put her tongue out and licked the sweet taste and breathed in deeply.

She was home.

*Part Six*

**The Year 2004**

# 1

## F is for Faith

A few mornings after moving in, Matilda looked in the mirror as she dressed in the room she now shared with Maggie. She could not help smiling. Life was for smiling about, wasn't it? What did she see in the mirror? A Beautiful Person. White shirt, palest tight blue jeans, healthy skin, thick loose hair. The glow of certain happiness.

She had come home. That was the weirdest feeling. Or rather, it was weird how natural it felt. It was as if nothing outside mattered. Nothing did. In here, up here, she was complete, moving as if on a warm breeze, blown gently along. She was accepted, part of this new family, brimful with belief.

P is for perfectly perfect. And pure.

And passionflower.

And Peter.

Everything before this time was nothing. Quite meaningless. All meaning was here. That was faith. Not questioning, because to question is to doubt.

Every now and then she tried to remember things from before, but they were vague and chill and unpleasant. Why had she stayed so long in the cold? Why stay in the cellar when the sun is streaming through the upstairs windows? She knew she had had parents, but they were part of another world now and they would understand the letter she knew she had written, even though she could not remember what it had said. And the people she had known before, who were they? The names were familiar – Cally, Jack, and earlier friends, and Matt, yes, Matt she remembered distantly, with a surprising apricot scent that came over her like a smile, but Matt was in a different place too. Matt didn't matter. All that mattered was here. She had already thrown away the two scraps of paper in her pocket. They were pointless pieces of the past.

She would try not even to think about the old things any more, the cold damp walls, the shadows. Here, everything was light and she had reached it.

Another hazy Saturday swollen with summer. The air was ripe and bursting. People walked limply. No breeze stirred the leaves. Matilda stood outside the greenhouses, looking down the hill. She saw the tiny people amongst the rows of fruit, picking slowly.

Up on the hill, the atmosphere had changed further over the last few days. Matilda had sensed it vaguely, though without concern. Perhaps it was the heat, the sense of summer peaking, of fruit past its best, beginning to wrinkle and desiccate. Up on the hill, people talked less, and often in huddled groups, or soft whispered comments in passing. There was more praying. Often Matilda would come across a couple of her new friends, standing with joined hands and tightly-shut eyes, in silent prayer, swaying softly together.

Perhaps it was the heat that sent Angel mad.

Matilda was standing there outside the greenhouse, enjoying a tiny breeze before going back in and finishing her job: checking tomato plants for greenfly. With a scrunch of gravel, Angel came running round from behind the greenhouse and pushed Matilda inside the door. Shut it after her. Dragged her towards the door into the next one, pulled out a swipecard and opened the door. 'Hurry, Matilda, hurry, hurry, please,' she was whispering frantically, gasping for breath.

Too shocked to react, Matilda allowed herself to be pulled. It all happened too quickly to wonder why. Angel threw the door shut after them.

And in the almost unbreathable heat of the middle greenhouse, Angel began to cry, her words utterly tangled by hysterical sobs. Matilda could make no sense of it. Half words, strangled syllables.

'Angel, hey, calm down, shhhh.' All she could do was try to calm the girl. Sweat glistened on Angel's forehead and her white shirt was stuck to her back and arms. It was too hot in here. Matilda wanted to get out, but she hadn't been given a swipecard. Only a very few of them had.

Slowly, Angel's sobbing calmed. She kept looking back through the first greenhouse, as if someone had been following her. Then her face twisted with fear again. Matilda looked. Two people, David and someone else, were running towards them. Angel grabbed Matilda's shoulders hard, hurting her with the rigid digging of her fingers, and through her wild-eyed sobs she forced these words, 'Get out! Just get out!'

The door swung open and David and another man rushed through. They pulled Angel away firmly, though not roughly, and the other man held her. 'Are you all right?' David asked Matilda, his arm on her shoulder, leading her away from Angel.

'Yeah, fine, fine, but what's going on? What's wrong with her?'

The other man had one arm round Angel, who was no longer struggling. She seemed quite limp, as though if he let her go she would fall. Her arms hung by their sides. The man led her away slowly, saying, 'It's OK now, Angel. Everything's OK. Give me the swipecard back, please.' In one hand he held a small brown bottle and he took the swipecard from her.

'What's wrong with her, David?' asked Matilda again.

'She'll be fine. She wasn't well before she came here. Mental illness. She's getting better, but she needs her pills and maybe she's not been taking them. I don't know. But she's fine now. Did she say anything to you?'

'She couldn't speak, she was so hysterical.'

'Nothing at all?'

'She just shouted that I had to get out. As though she hated me. But she was the one who dragged me in here, for goodness' sake!'

'Don't worry, Matilda. It's nothing personal. Just part of her illness. You did fine.'

David walked with her into the first greenhouse and then left her there, though she wanted him to stay and talk. She resumed her job checking for greenfly on the tomatoes. She felt sorry for Angel. The girl was clearly not well.

The morning drifted on in odd silence. Every now and then, Matilda went outside. No one else came to speak to her all morning. Once she saw a distant group walking along the terrace in front of the house. Peter was there. The man with the Jesus hair, as she used to call him. How beautiful he looked, and how full of peace.

He stopped. Placed both hands upon the head of one of his followers. She could see the smile spread across the girl's face, where before there had been something like worry. And then they walked on again, towards the greenhouse, towards Matilda.

As they came closer, she saw his features more clearly. The veil of corn-gold hair, the palest eyelashes, high cheekbones, the unusually dark pink lips. The colour, almost, of crushed raspberries.

Then he looked at her. Stopped and smiled at her. Straight at her. Raised his hand, palm towards her. She raised hers, too.

He walked on, with his followers, leaving behind the sweetest feeling melting through her. He only had to look at her for her to feel calm. The feeling of oddness disappeared and she simply relaxed into whatever the day would bring, stopped wondering.

# 2

## L is for Laughter and Lies

Evening. Dinner. All of them in their cleanest clothes. The elderflower wine. The smiles, the hugs, the greetings. But behind it all an air of something. Something intangible. Something waiting. The smiles a little too much. The hugs a little long. The greetings lingering in the eyes.

Matilda pushed the questions away again. *Be happy*, she told herself. *This is your home. Let it all happen. Don't spoil it or doubt it by asking questions. Let it enfold you.*

Peter coming into the room, moving through like warm breath, slowly approaching. Feeling him near her, sensing the air change and swell. And him passing behind her, speaking her name softly, *Matilda*. Turning round towards him and smiling at him. Hearing his words, 'Matilda, welcome. We are so glad to have you here. To stay with us. Well done, Matilda. Well done.'

And she knew she would die for him. She would do anything for him.

The laughter was louder tonight and she could see herself reflected in the sparkling faces of her friends, in their almost wildly happy eyes. Everything swirled round her like magic and she let herself be drawn into it, into the new mood of crazy abandon. There was dancing and singing and people hugging each other. She was faintly aware that this felt different from the last two Saturdays but she neither knew nor cared how or why. The difference was exciting, as if something special was about to happen.

As the meal came to an end, Peter stood up. Into the gathering silence he said, 'My followers, let us raise our glasses one last time.' She found her glass filled once more with the sweet red liquid. He smiled again, and his voice rose, calming the air around it. 'Drink together, my friends, and then let the word of God into your heart again.'

She drank and closed her eyes and gave up her body, swaying to the words as she let them into her and knew them again. As if they had been there inside her all along.

'Now let God arise, let His enemies be scattered. The righteous cry and the Lord heareth and delivereth them, delivereth them with fire into heaven. For only through fire shall they reach heaven. For the Lord loveth judgment and forsaketh not his saints; they are preserved

236

for ever; but the seed of the wicked shall be cut off. The Lord will save those who cry unto him and take them to his place of eternal peace.'

She felt His hands pass over her body, felt His words enter her heart and lift her towards heaven. She walked with Him through strawberry fields and laughed as she ran between the raspberry canes in the darkness. And as they all ran and laughed in the night, barefoot and free, they all knew they would die for Him.

and will have a chance to do good to them, and take them to
and His eternal Paradise.

# 3

## D is for Dancing and Danger

In the darkness, horrified eyes were watching. From behind a tree he stared. Saw people running and laughing crazily, carrying containers of something, spilling it everywhere. He watched them run down the hill away from the house, pouring the clear liquid as they went, on the lines of straw between the strawberries.

Petrol. It had to be.

George shrank behind the tree. He had seen enough. He had already seen them through the window, drinking too much. He had seen them raising their hands to the Jesus-figure, the man with the long hair, who obviously fancied himself as some new Messiah. He had seen them chanting, the same sentence over and over again, judging from their lips, but he couldn't make out what it was they were saying. And they must be drugged, must be. Otherwise why would they sway in front of the man like that and seem to worship him?

He had seen them dancing round that bowl of fire again, just as when he had looked before, watching Jemima. They did something with sticks that they dipped in the fire but he couldn't see that properly.

And now he could see them pouring what must be petrol over the strawberry plants. This was enough for the police. At last, it was enough. Excitement, and the pleasure of discovering that he had been right, took away some of his fear.

He had been right! He had always known they were a loony religious cult. It was obvious. But what about the petrol? What was that about? What was the point of setting fire to the strawberries?

A doubt crept in. Not that they were a loony religious cult – that was obvious. But was there anything wrong with burning their strawberry plants? Wasn't that what farmers did at the end of the season? OK, so it was odd, definitely odd to run about at night pouring petrol over strawberry plants, but was it illegal? Wouldn't the police just come along and ask a few questions and then these people would find some innocent answer to their questions.

He needed more.

George strained his ears and stared into the near darkness around him. Everyone still seemed to be down at the field. He looked towards the house. Lights were on downstairs, but there was no sign of anyone there, no movement in the windows that he could see. Quietly, he crept towards the house and edged his way round the back. The back door was slightly open. He listened again. Nothing. Tiptoed towards it. Peered through. No sound. He slipped in. Left or right? He chose to turn right, along a passageway and round the corner. A staircase, back stairs. Crept up, barely breathing.

A large landing, a dim orange light filtering from downstairs. Several passageways leading off it, at least eight doors closed on the landing itself. A large cross at one end, looming down at him.

A noise. He stood statue-still, unbreathing. A muffled crying. From where? He couldn't tell. Another noise. Downstairs. People. Talking. Coming nearer. He ran down one of the passageways. Near the end, a door was slightly open, no light showing.

He slipped inside.

The voices came closer. Stopped outside the door. Two people saying goodnight. One set of footsteps moving on.

The door opened.

# 4

## L is for Love

Matilda fell into bed still laughing. Her feet were wet from her barefoot running through the dew. As she lay there, her head span fantastically and she span with it, loving the feeling of letting go.

There were no shadows now. Wherever she looked inside her head everything was light.

L is for light. And Love. And Leaving behind. Letting go.

And Learning to Live.

Maggie turned to her now from the next bed and smiled a lazy smile. 'Are you happy, Matilda? Are you happy now? Do you see what I meant? That first day? In the greenhouse?'

'Yes, I know. I don't know why it worried me. I should have trusted you earlier.' Her lips felt thick and slow and dry. She licked them and tasted again the sweetness.

'And your brother? How do you feel about your brother now?'

'I love him.' No hatred. No jealousy. And a tiny tear formed, burst and trickled down her smiling face. 'I love him now.'

'And tomorrow?'

'Tomorrow?'

'Are you ready for tomorrow?'

Matilda didn't quite know what Maggie meant. 'Yes, of course.'

'And did you understand? Tonight. Everything? Why we are doing it? Why we love Peter and trust him?'

Matilda fought to remember what had happened that evening.

'I trust Peter. I love him. Of course.' The 'why' was somewhere deep inside. 'It's just something I know. That's faith, isn't it?'

Maggie smiled again. 'It will be all right, Matilda. Really. We will all be together. He will make it easy. For everyone. He will look after us. Because He loves us.' And Maggie lay back against the pillows and Matilda saw a tear shine on her cheek, too. It was the emotion of the evening, the traces of the drink, and what was in the drink, thought Matilda. The passionflowers. The extraordinary flowers from the last greenhouse and the glistening nectar which they milked each evening, and which turned red when it was blessed by Peter.

She loved how when a flower came to the end of its life, it was plucked, removing the seed head, so that no fruit would grow. All the goodness went to intensify the nectar in the other flowers.

Vaguely, Matilda knew that there was some hidden meaning in Maggie's words, a meaning which she ought to know. But the thought looked something like a shadow and she would have nothing more to do with shadows ever again.

Instead she made herself think of the beautiful twilight ceremony which she had been to three times now. Several of them would stand with Peter in the last greenhouse, in flickering candlelight, and would quietly pray as they held tiny glass vials below the ripest, most swollen passionflowers and watched the glistening drips fall. She loved the way each drip only fell when it was ready, when it was impossibly heavy, making gravity wait. And then how it cloyed to the sides of the glass, a silver snake slipping thickly and richly.

Then, when the passionflowers had stopped secreting their nectar and the night had completely fallen – for passionflowers reveal their deepest secrets to the moon – then Peter would bless the brimming vials as they held them high, with the blood-red petals reflected through the glass, and they would all walk silently back to the house, barefoot on the dew-drenched grass.

With these thoughts, she soon slipped away into sleep and a beautiful dream. All her dreams were beautiful here. Like the dreams she always thought she should have. She had been right to dream of perfection. She had been right all along.

# 5

## I is for Intruder

George lay rigid under the bed while he watched a pair of feet move backwards and forwards as their owner got ready for bed. Eventually, when he thought he could bear it no longer, the light was turned off and very soon he could hear the slow breathing of someone asleep. Giving one more minute to make sure, George slowly eased his muscles loose, rolled himself smoothly from under the bed and slipped out of the door.

The passageway was dark. Keeping close to the wall, he crept towards the stairs. Listened carefully – nothing. Only the loud tick of a clock and the occasional distant creak as the old house settled down for the night.

Trying not to think about the danger he was in, George crept down the stairs, wincing at every tiny squeak. Everyone was asleep. Deep in their alcoholic stupor, he hoped.

At the bottom of the stairs was an open door. He could see that it led into the main hall. He went through, more confidently now. There were six doors he could choose from. He didn't know what he was looking for so it didn't much matter which he chose.

He crossed the hall, keeping to the rug in the middle, taking large strides to minimise the chance of a creaking board. The first door led into a dining-room, with four long refectory tables sitting silent and dark, gleaming in the moonlight. Nothing interesting.

The next room was some sort of study, if the large desk was anything to go by. More interesting, thought George. He walked in. On the desk lay a large Bible, and a prayer book. Blank paper, pens, a clock, a cross, and a framed piece of yellowed card with the words, 'What must I do to be saved? Acts 30'.

He tried the drawers. All locked. George looked around. He walked over to a bookcase and was just about to read the titles when he heard a noise. A creak. From the hall. Heart thumping, he pulled open a door near him and slipped inside. Found himself in a huge walk-in cupboard. Pulled the door silently shut behind him. Stood entirely still, barely breathed. His heartbeat high in his throat. How could he have been so stupid? He should *never* have come here. Should have called the police. Or just done nothing. He wasn't the 'getting involved' type. For Christ's sake, why did he think he had to get involved now?

Matilda. But Matilda didn't care. She was lost already, wasn't she? Would she ever thank him for this? But he had had to act somehow. For her and Jemima and anyone else who might get caught up in this loony cult. He had tried to get the others interested. But they'd told him not to get involved. Matt was the only one who had really believed him, really been interested. And even when Matt disappeared, Jules and the others really didn't believe it was anything weird. Jules thought it was Matilda's fault. George *knew* it was more than that. He couldn't say how he knew, just that he watched people, noticed things, and the way some of the Beautiful People had behaved the day Matt disappeared was just odd. Maggie and David especially.

He listened. Thought he could hear footsteps come into the room. But he couldn't be sure. He would have to wait, for an hour if necessary. Till he was sure the person had gone.

He could see nothing in the cupboard. Could he risk his torch? Carefully, slowly, he pulled the small pencil torch from his pocket and, cupping it carefully with his hand, switched it on. There was no way it could be seen from outside the door. He moved the light around and followed its beam. It was too small to light up a large area but gradually he formed a picture of the cupboard. Shelves, dusty. With random objects. A few books, notebooks. Several mobile phones. The odd water bottle.

Mobile phones? Why? Why were they in here? Were these people not allowed to have mobile phones with them? He picked one up. He tried to switch it on – but it had no battery charge left.

He picked up another one. The same. And then another. This time, there was a small battery charge. And as the screen came to life, coldness swept over him when he read the words that appeared. 'Hello, Matilda!' It was the standard sign-on greeting from the phone company. As the sim card loaded itself, a flashing envelope indicated unread text messages. He had to open them. The first one was from several days ago.

'Hello M – we have not heard anything for a while. How are things? Love from Dad xx'

Then, 'Dear m – need to know you are ok. All well here. Love, Mumxxx'

'We really need to hear from you. Worried. Dad xx'

'Dear m, are you ok? Come on sweetheart, pls phone. Love you. Mumxxxxx'

'Dear Matilda, please contact us. We are worried. I am going away for few days. Please phone Mum – she is v worried. Dad xx.'

The last one was yesterday morning. Their worry was stark, horrible. George felt sick. No text today. Why didn't Matilda have her phone with her? And she should have contacted her parents. He couldn't bear to think of them not knowing how she was, or thinking she was ignoring them. Even Jemima had written to her parents and told them that she was going to stay with these people. And Jemima's parents had arrived the next day, trying to plead with her to come back. They didn't get very far, and bringing the police with them the following day got them nowhere – Jemima was an adult. If she chose to stay, no one could stop her, said the police. George remembered the look of desperation on their faces as they drove off.

He wished Matilda had written.

He switched the torch off and stood, listening for any sound outside. Nothing. Silently, he opened the door. Darkness, apart from the faint silvery glow from moonlight reflecting on the highly polished furniture. He pushed the door open wider and walked quietly out.

And crashed into blackness and a firework of spangled stars.

# 6

## P is for Passionflower Poison

It is Sunday. The Lord's day.

Matilda feels herself being dragged from sleep. Maggie is shaking her awake, looking down at her and smiling. 'Come, Matilda, it is time,' she says. 'Drink this,' and Matilda takes it but does not drink immediately. She makes herself wait.

If only her parents could see her now – her happiness – they would forgive her for choosing to live here, wouldn't they? They would understand. She remembers writing the letter, though she has forgotten what she wrote. And it was many days ago, so her parents will have received it by now, surely? Perhaps they have tried to phone her, though she thinks she told them not to, but she won't know because mobile phones are taken from all members. Rightly, Matilda knows. Communication with the past is unhealthy. It drags you with it; it holds you down. It stops you reaching the light. Move forward.

Now she drinks the tea Maggie brought. Passionflower and peach, of course. Matilda smiles blearily as she sips it.

Dimly in the distance, she hears people moving about. She looks at her watch but doesn't see it properly or care. Maggie tells her to get dressed and she does. She follows Maggie, holding her hand, dizzily and weirdly aware and unaware of what she is doing and why.

It is time. She knows that, somehow.

They meet others on the stairs, all going the same way, and Matilda knows and doesn't know who they are. Everyone is smiling, greeting each other, laughing.

No, not everyone. Some are crying, and being pulled gently by the others. Why are they crying, she wonders fleetingly? Angel is one of them, she sees. Inside herself, Matilda feels only warmth and soft peace. The tears on her face are from somewhere else entirely.

She hears them call each other, greeting each other. The name Jemima suddenly floats above the others. Jemima? She knows that name, remembers George talking about her. How she wishes George could be here now with all of them. She calls out Jemima's name and a tear-stained face gazes emptily back at her, the eyes glazed and powerless. Jemima is pulled gently away by someone, Rachel perhaps. Why is Jemima crying, Matilda wonders?

Down the stairs and outside, Matilda flies with the others, hardly knowing how she comes to be there. Past the perfect bay trees they run, linked together, past the salmon-pink geraniums and the herbs with the young sun blinking them awake. They crunch on the gravel and breathe the early morning sunshine through their nostrils. It is crisp and clean.

Her brother is in front of her, calling her name and holding out his arms to her, and she is running and laughing towards him. He leads her to the greenhouse. Everyone is there, moving from the first and into the second greenhouse and finally into the swollen heat of the last hothouse, among the red-robed flowers and the heady scent of the nectar and steam and familiar dreams. And all the time her brother, light all around his head, her brother with hair like Jesus', leading her.

She breathes in the steam and shuts her eyes, throwing her head back blissfully. Everyone crowds in and they swim into the heat together.

Peter stands tall beneath the passionflower trees, his eyes shut and arms open wide, drawing them all to him. To him they go, willingly and unwonderingly, and they laugh with him and love how he holds them each and all. And he gives them the sweet blood-red drink and they let it slide past their lips as he blesses them and they drift towards heaven together, towards the light. They drift and twist and float and cry and laugh all the while.

They kneel, they sink, they lie, they dream, they sleep. He wanders through them all as they lie there, blessing them as they begin their journeys. But they are not going yet, he knows that. For now, they know only an earthly peace and love, and it is for him to do the rest. All of them now, all of them are drifting together, going where he is taking them, and all are equal. The ones who were reluctant, the ones who doubted him, and the ones who doubted nothing, who had given everything up to him, and to God, his Father. All are the same now. Equal in God's eyes.

He is their Father now. And He must do what a Father must. 'He that spareth his rod hateth his son: but he that loveth him chasteneth him betimes.' He is only doing what He must.

The Father walks over to the wall and unscrews a metal cover, does what He must to the switches He finds there, feels a small tear at the corner of His eyes, wipes it away. Then the Father kneels and prays. Spearing pain shoots through His knees, but still He prays. His muscles twist into spasm, but He does not stop praying. Sweat runs down His back, trickles over His face, His clothes stick to Him, His head spins in the heat and the rising sun pounds onto the glass, but still the Father never stops loving His children and praying.

The blood–red passionflowers open their arms in the hothouse. They open their faces to the sun. They twist in ecstasy as the heat draws them up.

Beneath them the Father prays. He prays and prays and if He prays hard enough all will be forgiven. If He prays hard enough, the five wounds of the passionflower will bleed in the sunlight.

He will pray hard enough.

# 7

## A is for Apocalypse

George woke slowly to a sickening pain in his head. Everything was dark. He raised his head slightly. Aggghhh! He vomited. Sank back onto the cold damp floor again.

Closed his eyes. Span away.

Some time later – seconds or minutes, it was impossible to know – he woke again. Seeping through his head came vague memories, which quickly untangled themselves. The pain in his head swelled as he remembered what had happened. He struggled to sit up. Sickness came over him again and he stayed very still for a few moments till it passed.

He was in a cellar. He could tell by the ancient wet-earth smell. And it wasn't completely dark – greyish light was filtering through a window high up, so that he was gradually able to see more of his surroundings. Still a cellar. Some crates and containers of various shapes and sizes. Some tools leaning against a wall.

George tried to lick his lips but his tongue was sticking to the roof of his mouth. He desperately needed water, to get rid of the foul taste of vomit. But, more importantly, he had to get out of here. He didn't know what was going on but it was very obvious that his suspicions had been right. People don't get bashed on the head and thrown unconscious into a cellar if everything is above board, he knew.

Sitting up, he carefully touched his head, wincing as he did. Rubbed his fingers together. He didn't seem to be bleeding. He had heard of internal bleeding, and brain haemorrhage, but he put those thoughts away. No point in going there.

Slowly, like an old man, he forced himself to stand, steadied his legs. Fighting nausea, he straightened his neck. Better than he'd expected. He took a few steps towards the window. The dizziness was bad, but not unbearable. He could die in here if he didn't find a way out – that was the only thing to focus on.

At the window, he stretched up. A wooden shutter covered the space. He slid his fingers down each side and found a catch. Lifted it up, pulled the shutter towards him. Light flooded the cellar. Easy.

The sun was high in the sky. How long had he been unconscious? Where was everyone else? He listened, peering as far as he could through the small square window, the azure beyond. Nothing. No one to be seen or heard. It was a Sunday, of course, so there'd be no fruit-picking today, no need for the Beautiful People to go down to the farm.

The window had no glass, but it did have thick metal bars. He reached up. He could just manage to grip them. But they were solid. No hope of shifting them.

He leaned against the wall under the window.

Now what?

The door. George went over to it and turned the handle. It felt strong and the door looked heavy. He could probably smash it down eventually, but someone would hear him first.

Beginning to panic, George rummaged around amongst the boxes and containers, throwing each aside as it revealed nothing of use. Bottles of some sort of home-made wine, tinned food, gardening equipment, dusty seed packets, string, several boxes of screws and nails, random bits of nothing, ordinary objects. Nothing that was going to help him get out and save himself or anyone else from whatever it was that this loony religious cult was up to.

Where was everyone? Praying? Probably, he thought with an irritated sneer. He went over to the window again. Nothing. No one. He used a box to stand higher, to be able to put his whole face to the window. Utter silence. Just the sun rising higher in a boiling blue sky.

That was when he heard it. An explosion. Shattering the air. Screams of birds as they flew high into the sky. Another explosion. The screams of something else.

George picked up a spade from the pile of tools and smashed it against the door. He smashed and smashed, the metal glancing off the handle, off the iron studs, off the frame, flying everywhere. The spade broke, part of it hitting his shin. 'Shit!' he yelled. 'Shit!' He grabbed a fork. He screamed as he smashed, and screamed and smashed and smashed and screamed. And with one last huge effort he hurled himself at the door, feeling his shoulder crunching, his head spinning, sickness clogging his senses – and the door flew open.

George rushes, thoughts whirling, along the corridor, up the stairs at the end, flings open the unlocked door at the top and runs by blind instinct through the silent house and out through the back door. He can hear more explosions now. Breath painful in his throat, silently yelling, he flies towards the noise. The greenhouses. One of them destroyed already, its glass hanging and smithereened, the metal struts twisted around the carnage of plants. The misplaced smell of frying tomatoes. Flames dancing in a line along the ground, eating up the shrivelled leaves of slaughtered plants with a sizzling noise. Towards the second greenhouse.

He stands a little away, watching, empty-headed, his brain stunned, stone-like with shock.

He looks around, needing, needing, needing answers. Down the hill he looks. Flames, streams of fire. He stares. He tries to scream at what he sees but has no breath to spare. The man! The man with the fucking stupid Jesus hair is running through the strawberry fields and flames are snaking after him, flowing from his hands as he runs. The plastic poly-tunnels are shrivelling and shrinking into liquid, and George hears the distant shrieks of melons as they burst.

Another explosion. A slicing feeling on his cheek. He puts his fingers to his face. Blood. The second greenhouse. The melting smells of roasted peaches and grapes and a zillion shards of hot glass spray around him.

Where is everyone else? And then he hears the terrible screams. Looks back at the remaining greenhouse. Sees people running inside it, spiralling and twirling and burning. Fire! Inside the glasshouse. He begins to rush towards it, towards the people screaming. He sees crazy splashes of red amongst the branches and arms, sees the orange flames licking upwards, sees the shrivelling dying plants tumble, twisting down before the greenhouse explodes into a huge blood-red fireball and glass scatters everywhere. The air is pushed from his lungs and the heat leaps towards him.

He tries to run. He tries. But his legs have lost their power. He sinks to his knees. And amongst the screams and the running stumbling arm-waving shattered people, the staccato explosions and rivers of fire running up the hill towards the house, and the man with the Jesus hair standing in the flaming field and praying – amongst all that, George hears something else.

Behind him, a car screeching to a gravelled halt by the house. He turns, as if in slow motion, confused by so many shocking things, so much noise and pain. He sees, in all this chaos, the car, gleaming despite the dustiness of its wheels, proud and new in its state-of-the-art glory, a strawberry red . . . what was it called? He had seen the adverts, heard the hype – yes! A Branson Mirage. And stepping out of it, with neat ankles and smart Sunday clothes – because it is Sunday, of course – a woman.

A little middle-aged woman with an expensive handbag, and exclusive shoes from somewhere chic and a neat designer suit, and once-perfect hair and starkly pale cheeks and manicured fingers. In all the chaos, every pointless detail screams out to George. It is as if time has stopped and then shattered into separate bits and in each bit he has endless time to wonder and look and understand who this woman is and why she is there.

And then the little middle-aged woman screams. She screams one word, 'Matilda!'

*Part Seven*

# The Year 2029

# 1

## J is for Judgement

Now she would have to be stronger still, she would, the little old woman with the failing heart and never-fading will. She would have to be hard and strong and cold and brutal. She would have to have a hardness in her. She had come this far and she had not failed. She would not fail now.

She would not fail her daughter now. She had failed her before, arriving too late in response to her daughter's shocking letter. The letter which, in the years after that day, she had read and reread, and wondered at the unknowable reason why it wasn't posted until many days after it was written. Was it deliberate or accidental? She would never know because Matilda didn't know, and they had talked of it often since then. All those years ago, but the words of the letter still a half-healed wound in a mother's mind. The words that told her, with painful and brutal truth, how she had hurt her daughter with her blind grief.

How she had damaged her and driven her away.

But when she had read the letter that terrible day, had she not frantically cancelled the charity lunch she had been getting ready for, and leaped straight into her brand new red sports car – impulsively bought after her daughter had left home, the much-hyped car designed for younger, freer women, bought despite (or perhaps because of) her husband's exasperated and uncomprehending disapproval? Had she not stopped only to phone her husband on his faraway golf weekend and had she not driven through clogged Saturday motorways, and then through the night, sleeping briefly in a service station when even fear would not keep her eyes open? Had she not done all this, desperately trying to catch her falling daughter? To tell her she was sorry, to tell her she loved her – always had – but was just too . . . too frightened to show it? Because it had seemed that, if you love something too much, God is angered.

Had she not shown her love ever since? Once she had recovered – somewhat – from the sickness of her double grief, and once she had seen how to atone? Had she not shown it in her careful planning over the last few years? Carefully she had planned, she had, telling no one, not her husband, not anyone – not even God – of her crippled faith. Caressing secrets inside her, nurturing the strength she would need when the time came. Because one thing she had always known: that he would never be free. Never, the man with the stupid Jesus hair and the nasty flat feathery fingers and his hateful smile and his sickly-sweet vanilla voice.

She had saved his soul, of course she had. She had saved his soul for herself. To save herself. She had deceived even God. She had deceived everyone. She grinned, grinned she did, the little old woman with the neat, obedient hair and the expensive bag from Bond Street. To think that anyone could have thought she was merely a nice little old woman, a tea-drinking, neatly-dressed, empty-headed, well-meaning, fragile old bat! To think that anyone would think she actually believed in the power of God's healing! And forgiveness!

Forgiveness! Pah! It was God's ridiculous insistence on forgiving that had turned her against Him in the first place. Never forgive! Never.

So she had hidden her heart from God. She had lied. She had even lied about her doubts. In thought, word and deed she had lied. She had promised that God could judge and forgive and have Peter's soul. And God had believed her.

And now, at last, she gripped once more the bruised steering-wheel of her twenty-five-year-old Branson

Mirage. It had served her well: for twenty-five years she had enjoyed the confusion in people's eyes when they tried to link this ordinary-looking woman with such an extraordinary car. It shouted, as she had so often wanted to do, 'Look at me – I have a spirit too!' Nearing the end of its life now, it was. As she was hers. Her aching heart and her increasing dizziness told her so. She hadn't been to the doctor or consulted the Compudoc again. There really hardly seemed any point.

She drove fast to the meeting-place. She kept the roof closed, her hair neat. The car purred beneath her, breathing with her. Autumn reds bathed the nearby trees and a few white clouds scudded over the huge sky. The weak sun was struggling to warm the air. A double string of geese sailed across the blue emptiness towards another place.

At a Juice 'n' Jeans, the so-called 'lifestyle bar' on the edge of a town, more than seventy kilometres from her own house, she smoothed the car to a stop. Looked around. No sign of him. She relaxed, leaning back in the familiar faded squishtic, and waited, breathing deeply, needing the oxygen. A tiny crackle of pain shot again across her chest, down her arm. Then disappeared. She breathed easily once more.

A tapping on the passenger window. She controlled herself before she opened her eyes, holding on to herself for the feeling she knew would come. How seeing him cracked the breath in her chest. She opened her eyes. His face, his smiling face, her uncoiling hatred.

She pressed the button to lower the window.

'Sarah! How wonderful to see you.'

'Peter,' she greeted him, smiling. 'Get in.'

He spoke through the window. 'I thought we might have something here, in the café – juice bar or whatever you call it. I wanted to treat you. Before we go and view the house. We have time.'

'I know a better place, Peter. You can still treat me. Get in.'

He climbed in. Turned to look at her, held out his hands for hers. She didn't want to touch him, but she had no choice.

This was the first time she had touched him. Her skin recoiled. His hands were clammy, soft, unnaturally soft. She looked down, away from his staring eyes. She didn't like the way he wore jeans. He was too old for jeans. Pale blue jeans and a white shirt. Far too old. And too old for such long hair too. Still that creepy hair, like a hippy, she thought. An aging hippy. But a dangerous one, still. She must be careful.

'Sarah, it's so good to see you. Thank you for answering my message, and for coming.'

He held her a little longer, touching the ugly

273

diamonds, holding such wealth in his hands. How he wished he could have given these diamonds to his mother. If only she had lived and not this ugly rich witch. Still, he would use her wealth.

'Shall we go, Peter?' said the little old woman sweetly. 'We should be getting going, if we are to have some refreshment before we visit the property.'

Peter did his seatbelt up as she released the clutch, and they set off. They drove west across the moors, towards the falling autumn evening sun. The little old woman put on her sunglasses. 'Let's have the roof down, shall we, Peter? Let us really enjoy ourselves. We should celebrate your freedom.' And she pressed the button which let the roof slide back with little more than a wheeze.

And the woman pulled a long pin out of her hair and let it fall free, shaking it around her head and accelerating till it streamed behind her like smoke. She grinned again. And Peter looked at her and grinned too, mistaking her heartsong for happiness.

For a while there was only the sound of the wind in their ears above the smooth purring of the car's engine. West they drove, fast, faster than little old women usually drive. But then this was no usual little old woman.

Peter looked over to her. He saw again her wrinkled

gecko-eyes, her downy, dry, corrugated skin, her ashen hair. But now, for the first time, he saw the light in her eyes, saw fire, saw passion. And he wondered briefly at her, at her strangeness.

He did not wonder for long. The car slowed suddenly, almost skidding as it turned sharp left. Down a track. There had been a sign, a notice, but Peter hadn't seen what it said.

The old woman had seen what it said. She knew. This was why she was here. This was what everything had led up to. The sign had said, 'No entry. Caution. Disused quarry.'

Along the stony track the woman pounded her dying red sports car. It screamed in protest. She fought to control its speed along the winding and rock-strewn path. Faster and faster she drove, her face set hard.

'Sarah! What are you doing? Slow down! You'll damage the car!' Peter shouted above the shrieking engine. He clutched the dashboard with both hands.

You had to harden your heart, you did. You had to have much more than a touch of hardness. The woman stared straight ahead, her jaw rigid, her eyes narrowed. She would not be swayed now. She would not be manipulated. This was where it would all end.

In the distance they could both see the gaping nothingness of the quarry. A thin line, like lips slightly open in mild surprise. Closer and closer it came, jaws opening. Faster and faster the car skidded and scraped over the track.

With supreme and practised skill, the little old woman with the tired heart, and the not-so-weak will, applied the brake firmly, bringing the car skidding almost to a halt a few feet from the edge. Then, in first gear, she edged it forward smoothly again, very slowly and very purposefully, the toes of her right foot gently squeezing the tiniest amount of power from the engine, the toes of her left foot carefully preventing the car from stalling. She turned and looked at Peter as she did.

Eyes wide in terror, only just beginning to understand, he shouted at her, 'No! Please, Sarah! I don't know what's wrong but, please! Stop the car!'

'Why, Peter?' she said, coolly, a tiny fleck of white spittle at the corner of her lips. Her lipstick had formed into a sticky-slappy ridge. She didn't care. 'Tell me why?'

He didn't answer. She looked at him, still edging the car forward inch by inch, revolution by revolution. He was crying. The man with the Jesus hair and the buttery lashes and the palest blue eyes, the feathery fingers, the man with the sick and evil heart, was crying!

She stopped the car. It must be only inches from the

edge. She did not put the handbrake on. She kept her feet balanced perfectly on the clutch and the accelerator, holding the car steady on the fraction of a muscle movement. It would take the tiniest adjustment for it to shoot forwards over the edge. A single twitch would do it. The quarry lay open before them, its emptiness and its space breathtakingly deep.

'You're crying, Peter? *You're* crying? Don't you think it should be me crying, not you? And don't you think that it's a little late for crying?'

He put his face in his hands.

He will try to manipulate you, they had said. He will do everything in his power. Well, who had the power now? The Jesus man or the little old lady with the tired heart?

She felt a twinge of pain across her chest again. Spangles across her eyes. She blinked.

Peter spoke, no longer crying. His voice was quiet. And he looked at her, with something like pity. And fear? Surely there must be fear there too? She wanted that. He had to suffer.

'I understand now,' he said. 'You lied to me, didn't you? You told me you didn't have children. I felt your pain when you told me – I saw it in your eyes. But I got it wrong, didn't I? I thought you meant you had *never* had children. But you lost someone, didn't you? At the farm?' He was trying to speak calmly, she could tell, trying to distract her. Perhaps thinking he could sway her.

She made no movement of her head, said nothing. Kept her feet steady with difficulty. Her eyes began to blur and the dizziness grew. It was difficult to hold the car still, to concentrate enough. She looked ahead, at the quarry.

'Who was it? Who did you lose, Sarah?' His voice so gentle, so kind, as though he would wrap her up in it, as though he would make everything all right with his smooth, milky voice. And perhaps he could. He could manipulate her, if she let him. Perhaps she should. After all. She could almost believe he could make it all right, when he spoke so softly.

'Who was it, Sarah? I am so sorry. Really so sorry. But I have paid, and I am still trying to pay. Who did you lose?'

'Don't manipulate me, Peter. You've tried to do it before. Don't do it now.' Still she looked straight ahead, hardened herself again, did not meet his eyes, focused on keeping her feet steady, her mind clear.

'I want to help you, Sarah.'

'You deserve to die, Peter. It is very, very simple. It always has been.' A strange small tear ran down her check.

' "The day of death is better than the day of one's birth." '

'Ecclesiastes.'

'Well done, Sarah. Very impressive.'

He stopped talking. She waited for him to say something else. What was she waiting for? For him to try to save himself? For the right moment to press the accelerator and release the clutch? It was becoming harder to concentrate. Her calf muscles were becoming cramped. Pain shot again across her chest, and then disappeared. The silence grew. Only their breathing and the tiny impatient purring of the car beneath them.

She had waited for this moment, had planned every second of it. Except that she realised there was one thing she had not thought about. Something simple, but surprisingly important: would she shut her eyes at the last moment or would she keep them wide open? It was not an easy decision.

Still the silence. Peter was saying nothing. He was not begging or trying to talk her out of it, not trying to persuade her to reverse the car. What was he doing?

She looked towards him. His eyes were closed and his lips were flickering very slightly. He was praying!

*No! No, he must not pray!*

'No! God doesn't want you, Peter! He does not forgive you!'

And, with the tiniest muscle movements of her legs, she released the car and it flew forwards into the void.

Peter smiled at her as they fell. And with a bursting pain of joy splintering her chest, she took him with her into beautiful oblivion.

# 2

# R is for Revelation

The doorbell rang. Matilda looked out of the window and smiled. He was here, as arranged. She walked slowly down the stairs. Stairs were always hard. One day she would sell this house, when her mother no longer needed her, and she would move to somewhere easy and new, a bungalow by the sea, perhaps. Maybe with a huge verandah or conservatory where she could sit in a traditional rocking chair and gaze out over endless waves and see no trees or hills or rows of anything. She hated rows of anything.

Matilda opened the door and George came in. Same old George, even though she hadn't seen him for nearly a year. He looked at her, smiled, held out his arms and they hugged. She managed not to wince when the skin on her back stretched. She led him through to the other side of the house and they made tea in the old-fashioned way and sliced the rich gooey fruit-cake.

He tried to do everything for her but she brushed aside his concern. The way she walked looked so painful, he thought. Yet she smiled and chatted like someone who was not in pain.

When they were sitting down, in the large conservatory where Matilda's mother grew her flowers, George looked around him and through to the rambling garden. It was a perfect setting for a peaceful life, he thought, a safe life away from people staring and wanting to ask questions. Matilda and her mother had created a dream out of horror. He smiled. Her friends said Matilda always had been a dreamer, always had wanted perfection. Well, in a strange way she had it now.

He looked at her, at her thick hair pushed back behind one ear. On the other side, hair fell over her face. The side that was always turned tactfully away from whoever was with her, so that at first you might think there was nothing wrong. She kept her hair quite long, when most women her age did not.

George leaned forward. She let him push the hair behind her other ear, smiled gently at him, looking straight at his eyes. His eyes never wavered, though every time he saw the terrible twisted scars he had to remember that awful day and the screams and the bursting fruits and flying glass and the heart-wrecking

282

sounds of people burning. The smell of roasting fruit would be with him for ever.

'It's great to see you. Thanks for coming, George.'

'It's great to see you too. Have you heard anything?'

'No, I expect it'll be on the news later. I won't watch. It doesn't make any difference to me. That he's out. I have my own life. My friends. You. Even though you live so far away.'

'But you could come and live with me, Matilda. You know . . .'

'I know, George, but the answer's still the same. While my mother is still alive, still needs me, I'll stay with her. She might seem OK a lot of the time, but . . . One day, maybe, who knows?'

George gently stroked her wrecked face. She smiled at his sensible clothes, his tidy mid-brown hair with already a few neat grey flecks, his lightly-lined face. He was safe, George was, and how she loved his safeness now. How out of place he looked amongst the vibrant red passionflowers her mother grew. When he had first come to this house, five years ago when Matilda and her mother had moved down south after her father's death, George had been shocked by the flowers. Before, in Scotland, when her mother had been learning how to grow them, practising and then cultivating just the right strain, she'd grown them in the greenhouse at the bottom of the garden and he'd never seen them on his visits. Now she grew them in the conservatory. Closer to her.

'Is that sensible, Matilda?' he had whispered when her mother had gone off to boil the kettle, that first time he saw them.

'Don't worry, George. I'm OK with them,' she had said. 'I know you find this hard but they gave me something. And Peter did, you know. No, don't,' she had added hurriedly, as his face darkened into anger, 'George, don't be angry. Please, understand. He saved me. He gave me back my brother and he saved me from . . . I suppose myself. And the passionflowers were part of that.' And eventually, after many more conversations like this, sometimes late into the night, sometimes walking through woods and fields, George had had to accept that out of evil, true evil, had come some good.

If George and Matilda had accepted, Matilda's mother never could. For a while, it was as though she had wanted to kill Peter, to rip him apart with her bare hands. George remembered how she had screamed and had to be restrained when the doctor had told them that Matilda had been pregnant and that the nature of her injuries meant she never would be again. George remembered too, how Sarah had at first, briefly, blamed him for that, until she realised that he was Matilda's friend and would never hurt her. And George and Sarah had eventually grown to like each other, and to understand each other. Now, he never talked to Sarah about what had happened all those years ago, though he knew she had never forgotten. You could see it in her eyes sometimes. Her love for her daughter and her hatred of Peter. But Matilda and her mother had built something important between them and George knew that was good for Matilda. He would do anything for Matilda, always would, and that meant he would wait for her.

'Where is your mother?' asked George now.

'I don't know. She plays bridge every Tuesday afternoon. Has done for weeks. It's helped her a lot – you can tell how she looks forward to it. She's usually back by now, though.' She looked at her watch but didn't worry too much. It was good to have George to herself, without her mother fussing.

George and Matilda talked and laughed and discussed ordinary things – holidays, the weather, traffic, the government, work – as they waited for her mother to return.

As the day turned into evening, the passionflowers in the conservatory slowly seeped, each heavy bead hanging, teasing gravity. Behind them, a deep sunset bled across the sky, turning the nectar red as blood. A little later, a soft pale moon appeared and, when it did so, a breeze, perhaps a draught from somewhere, gently shook the flowers and the drips fell at last.

But the little old woman was not there to catch them.

# Latest News from World On-Line
# MASS MURDERER IN DOUBLE DEATH-DIVE

Wednesday 13 September

Peter Johnson, the convicted mass-murderer and cult leader, was found dead in a car yesterday with the mother of one of the survivors of his mass suicide pact, which claimed the lives of 34 young people just over 25 years ago. Johnson, 54, had been released from prison the same day. The dead woman, Sarah Nailor, 73, who was allegedly driving the car, had been visiting Johnson in prison for several months and the authorities are investigating how someone connected to the original case could have been allowed to be his Volunteer Friend. 'We obviously had no idea who she was,' said a spokesperson for the prison. 'Our systems are meant to prevent such things. We are investigating how she could have deceived us. She even changed her name.' The car was found at the bottom of a disused quarry 70 km away.

Nailor's daughter, Matilda, now 43, was badly injured in the fatal pact at Apple Tree Farm near Ashburton, Dartmoor, almost dying of third-degree burns and internal injuries, from which she never completely recovered. Nailor's husband died five years ago and the couple also lost a son to cancer, aged eight. A local resident, who did not want to be named, said, 'It's a terrible story. She was always a bit odd, but she seemed harmless enough. We all thought she was just a nice little old lady who had been through a lot.'

Johnson was the leader of a religious cult, the Garden of Eden. Forty-three cult members were involved in the suicide pact and 34 died in the greenhouses, which had been doused in petrol before being set alight by an elaborate system of detonators throughout the farm. Johnson had drugged cult members with a substance distilled from a rare passionflower. Johnson was also convicted of conspiracy to murder Matthew Davidson, 22, a young freelance reporter whose remains were found buried in the garden with all his possessions, including the mobile phone which identified him.

Locals are speculating about how the car came to make its fatal plunge to the bottom of the quarry. Some believe that Johnson took her with him on a final suicide pact, while others believe it was a plot by a deranged Nailor to avenge her daughter's terrible injuries.

Police are keeping an open mind. An inquiry will be held.